Ito-san

MARC RIGAUDIS

Ito-san

Stories

Translated from the French and with an Introduction by

JAMES KIRKUP

PETER OWEN

LONDON & CHESTER SPRINGS PA

PETER OWEN PUBLISHERS
73 Kenway Road London SW5 0RE
Peter Owen books are distributed in the USA by
Dufour Editions Inc. Chester Springs PA 19425–0449

Translated from the French *Ito-san*

This edition first published in Great Britain 1991

British Library Cataloguing in Publication Data
Rigaudis, Marc
Ito-san.
I. Title
843.914

ISBN 0–7206–0818–X

Printed in Great Britain by Billings of Worcester

Contents

Acknowledgement

Parts of the Introduction have previously appeared in *The Times Literary Supplement* and *The Asahi Evening News*.

The explanatory footnotes were for the most part written by the translator.

Introduction

Great nations show themselves at their best in adversity. Success in war, whether military or economic, may bring them material glory and comfort, but failure enriches the soul. Prosperity can kill the soul of a nation. We can take as examples French and British colonialism and racial domination in Africa, India, South-East Asia. The British colonial bully is still with us, though he belongs to a dying race. In more recent times the image of the 'Ugly American' in the Far East is now fortunately almost a figure of the past.

It may truly be said that Japan is a great nation, and one that shows herself at her best particularly in adversity, whatever form that may take – defeat in war, nuclear holocausts, foreign occupation, natural catastrophes, universal condemnation for past atrocities in Korea, China, Malaysia, Burma. Even today, at the height of her economic success, Japan still exhibits nobility in adversity whenever an earthquake, typhoon or tidal wave strikes her islands, as I have often witnessed with my own eyes. It is then that the social homogeneity, the cultural uniformity and the native organizational genius are employed to their best ends. That such human skills and material help are not always extended promptly and unequivocally to other nations in distress is a regrettable peculiarity of Japanese diplomatic perception and of a governmental machine always slow and cautious in reaction to demands from the outside world – a disparity of humanitarian effort that is now gradually being overcome.

Japan today is undoubtedly one of the great economic giants of the modern world. She has worked and struggled hard to attain this well-deserved success, gained against all odds. Yet economic triumphs, financial security and international diplomatic status are not everything, as some Japanese have begun to realize. Prosperity has often been won at the expense of individuality; social conformity at the expense of love. Almost total literacy has been achieved at the expense of freedom for children to create, to use imagination, to learn initiative, to stray from the norm; to succeed in booming Japan, one cannot be that 'outsider' in Japanese society, someone 'different' from everyone else, a foreigner, an alien, a social outcast, a victim of nuclear radiation diseases, a half-caste, an 'untouchable'. It is in these areas that today's Japan exhibits the flaws and drawbacks of material success, of lifelong employment and financial plenty for all those who toe the expected line. Japan rejects the original, the individual, in favour of the stereotyped, the group. The Japanese often denounce 'difference' as 'arrogance' and 'egotism' – the severest criticisms a Japanese can make of his fellow-men who prefer to go their own way in life.

It is against this frightening background of monotonous social conformity and standardized daily existence that Marc Rigaudis has composed his remarkable collection of short stories. His style is plain, direct, unsparing; his themes are far removed from the usual rose-tinted views of Japan produced by casual visitors and diligently promoted by guide-books, television travelogues and official organizations like the Japan Travel Bureau. It is significant that in recent advertisements by the Japanese Ministry of Education calling for foreign volunteers to teach on short contracts in schools, what is stressed is that applicants should never have worked in Japan before. Such temporary newcomers can nearly always be relied upon to take back home with them, along with their souvenirs, the expected, idealized picture of life in Japan. People who know Japan too well are not to be trusted, and indeed all foreigners are not to be trusted, as we find in some of these stories.

Marc Rigaudis knows Japan well – too well. His stories are full of unhappy foreigners, and even more unhappy Japanese. A number of what might be called 'Ugly Japanese' appear in 'Samurai', 'All for My Child or Noriko', 'The Contract' and especially in 'She Was So Pretty'. In the last-named story, 'gangster' high-school girls torment a classmate because her exceptional beauty makes her 'different', and in the end send her to her death by composing a 'joke obituary' for her, signed by her classmates and their teacher. This story is based on an actual incident, one of hundreds involving the suicide of children every year. Rigaudis has an interesting comment on the 'gangster' persecutors: he says they are trying to break their chains. In 'The Contract' an American striptease dancer of majestic loveliness falls into the hands of *yakuza* or professional gangsters, and into the hands of a sex maniac, from whom she escapes by the skin of her teeth. This story is also based on fact, on the callous murder of a Dutch girl in Paris by the rich young Japanese student Sagawa, who chopped her up and ate several portions of the body which he kept in his refrigerator. The atmosphere of terror and nervous dread in this story will be familiar to all those who have lived for long periods in Japan. Sagawa was soon set free, and wrote a best-seller about his experiences in a bizarre form of self-defence. He can sometimes be seen strolling through the midnight streets of Tokyo's entertainment districts, where he has become a kind of star. In 'The Contract' the only person who treats the stripteaser decently is a small-time gangster who recruited her in the United States. The men who come to gape at her glorious nudity and who are 'serviced' by her in public on the open stage are depicted as anonymous morons or big babies.

The theme of the Japanese as 'big babies' is well developed in 'Ito-san' and particularly in 'All for My Child or Noriko', in which an ambitious mother, the kind the Japanese call 'Education Mamma', works hard all her life to make her son a success by getting him to pass the entrance examination to 'prestigious' Tokyo University. When this lusty young adolescent begins showing strong sexual urges, the mother is terrified lest sex will conquer all and ruin her plans. So after long thought, in order to keep her boy at his rote studies and memorization tests, she decides she must 'service' him to keep him quiet, just as she occasionally 'services' her indifferent husband – by fellatio, it is implied. This story is also based on common incestuous experiences among the Japanese, who in a prudish, moralistic and censorious society can find sexual release only in the privacy of their own families, or in the commonly accepted 'love hotels' or houses of assignation.

All these stories show Japan at her contemporary worst. There are very few redeeming features. Most of the stories tell of the horrors of being 'different' in a conformist, rigidly exclusive society in which it is painful for any kind of outsider to exist – especially the foreigner. This is best expressed in 'Samurai', in which an unhappy, frustrated young Swedish male model sinks slowly into suicidal depression and drug-taking – one of the most serious offences in Japan. In the end, David commits suicide. Ito-san becomes the first case of Aids registered in Japan, a land that thinks only foreigners catch the disease. The striptease dancer Lina and the Swedish model David are good-looking, but their beauty is useless in Japan, and that is why they, and so many other foreigners and 'different' Japanese, come to feel they are suffocating in the monotonous exclusivity of Japanese life. This is how David expresses it to his model friend Elizabeth:

> The country, these people, they get on your nerves. You cannot say why, but that's how it is. He has tried to explain his feelings to his friend Kris, who has just arrived from Sweden, but Kris couldn't understand why he was up in arms against such nice people. 'They are so kind and polite. The girls laugh all the time. And they're so sweet. . . .' Kris has just stepped off the plane. It's useless to try explaining to someone who has just stepped off the plane. More than in any other land, society here oppresses him, makes him feel he is suffocating. And as if in some bad dream he is sinking deeper, he cannot extricate himself from this glutinous mass that is closing over his head.

When we read such passages in Rigaudis's realistic and truthful tales, we understand why the Japanese Ministry of Education prefers short-time teachers who have 'just stepped off the plane'.

The unhappy state of Japan at present is also a kind of adversity, though few people, and even fewer politicians, realize it. We can only hope that this, too, will one day bring out the best in the Japanese, and make their land once more a pleasant place to live in.

Tokyo James Kirkup

Ito-san

Ito-san gets out of his black limousine, head lowered, and does not even think of raising it, contrary to his custom. Nor does he think of throwing out his chest as he has always done, all his life. He enters the hospital by a little side door and follows the arrows pointing the way to 'Analyses Bureau'. Labyrinth of long corridors with here and there some chairs arranged on either side of an open door. People sitting on some of these chairs, mostly old people looking morose. Ito-san notices that they all hold a yellowish card on which one can make out, in big black characters, a number. Round a corner of a corridor Ito-san stops in front of a large sign saying 'Analyses Bureau'. To the left of the sign, an open door; below the sign, a few empty chairs. Ito-san enters. At once a nurse seated at a minuscule desk lifts her head and looks at him with a questioning air. In a harsh tone of voice Ito-san brings out: 'My name is Ito . . . I received a telephone call from. . . .' The young woman does not let him finish, stands up and, her face wearing an impassive expression, signals to him to follow her. Two or three rooms cluttered with strange, hostile machines, bathed in a whitish atmosphere with an acrid and sickening smell. They come to a white door. No name on it. Nothing on the wall either. An immense white wall, completely bare. Beside the door, a tiny bench, all white too. Ito gazes at it fixedly as if completely absorbed by that ridiculous piece of furniture.

He realizes he is being invited to sit down there to wait awhile. Ito is about to sit down, but already the door opens and he is invited to enter. In front of him, an enormous desk, and behind the desk, ensconced in an armchair of black imitation leather whose back seems too high, sits a little grey-haired man. His eyes behind the glasses that break up the light into numberless facets are but two black streaks. All the lines of his still-smooth face descend towards the corners of his lips to form a sort of semi-parenthesis. The stringy neck resembles that of a tortoise. . . .

Ito-san opened his newspaper at the sports page and began to read the report on last night's baseball match. He read it without passion, somewhat automatically. Ito-san had a horror of passion. In the evenings, after his bath, sipping a beer, he would watch blankly television programmes in which people were shown laughing, weeping, shouting, people loving each other, detesting each other. . . . Ito-san watched all that without the least spark of comprehension, compassion. His impermeability to all the problems of those little characters jerking about in front of him was total.

His own life had from the start proceeded so comfortably! Its well-oiled, well-regulated gears had meshed of their own accord.

Only the memory of his mother remained with him from his childhood. His mother – young, always present at his side. Always there to wipe his hands with an immaculate handkerchief as soon as they happened to come in contact with earth, sand, stones in the park. They would often go and spend a few hours, whole days of sun, in a little park quite close to their home. Other children soon became a kind of menace, too often disrupting the little boy's habits with their inconsiderate actions, all the more unpredictable because he found them incomprehensible. Very soon he discovered that his mother's world was the one that suited him best and he always made every effort to remain within it as much as possible. School might have put a brake on this way of thinking. Those long hours of separation, away from the nest of home, seemed unendurable to him. But very quickly Ito-san was able to rediscover in that environment a maternal essence. All he had to do was to remain within his group, to let himself be borne along, cradled, guided by a list of regulations that formed a protective framework for him. Perfect acceptance of what is done and of what is not done guaranteed the security of young Ito, of whom all that was expected was that he should follow as correctly as possible a well-marked path encumbered with obstacles for which he was prepared in a way that left nothing, or almost nothing, to chance.

In this manner he ascended, after much hard work, effort and abnegation, the various steps that led him without problems to a prestigious university. The four years spent at university had almost constituted a threat to young Ito's equilibrium. Too much free time and too much liberty. Although he did not cut a single class and although his own work took up a part of his days, he still found himself left with a lot of leisure time to be filled in at his own discretion. This problem was beginning to weigh unpleasantly upon the nervous system of young Ito when he was approached by Tanaka-san. Tanaka-san was just a little shorter than he, and just a little plumper. He wore the same kind of spectacles as Ito-san and the same kind of hair-style, a sort of stiff-brush cut that was very practical because it made the use of a comb quite unnecessary.

Ito-san had already noticed him in the lectures on European civilization, during which they both were often to be seen diligently snoozing on benches a little distant from each other.

One fine day Tanaka-san introduced himself to Ito-san and asked if he could spare him a few minutes. A little confused by such direct contact, Ito-san muttered that he was free at the moment. That was when the young fellow-student proposed that he should join the FOB or Friends of Butterflies club, with a membership of three (they were never more than five). The club offered organized expeditions in springtime to hunt those graceful insects, then put them in formalin, classify and catalogue them. So the greater part of their activities consisted of looking up Latin names in big dictionaries and in writing those names under the corpses of the little creatures on their pins, keeping registers and classifying and cataloguing them.

Ito-san was at once excited by the idea but replied that he would give his answer after thinking it over for a while. So Ito-san's days at the university became very full. Thanks to the FOB, Ito-san was able to get through his university years without any problem, and above all without having to wonder where he was going.

Then came his entry into the company he was never to leave. How overjoyed his mother was when he had put on his brand-new navy-blue suit in order to go to his office for the first time! He had read in her eyes all the pride of a wife who has done her duty. He even remembered that look with a certain embarrassment. He could not have said exactly why, but that uncustomary display of emotion had at the time somewhat disturbed him.

Then came the monotonous succession of day after day, interrupted only by his first promotion, then by his marriage, then by other promotions, each one as regular and expected as the others. In fact, once his position in the firm had been established, his mother had asked him to meet a very suitable young lady, the daughter of one of her friends. The wedding had been arranged for the following year. His wife, exemplary in every way, had given him two children, first a girl and, three years later, a boy. His daughter, now aged fifteen, had the same placid, indifferent attitude to life as her father. Her plain face always looked worried, but actually her only worry was to lead a life without any problems. She enjoyed her food and was very fat for a girl of her age. Ito's son showed an unexpected and disturbing liveliness. Often his father looked at him as he would have at a stranger, so shocked was he by his attitude. He did not content himself with just reading the sports page in the newspaper: his whole life seemed to be devoted to baseball, and he would come home from the local sports ground covered with dirt, his cheeks glowing from the fresh air and looking happy. So much liveliness disgusted Ito-san. It was, quite simply, indecent.

Ito-san had found a seat on the train, and was sitting with straight back, knees well spread, exhibiting with a kind of obscene frankness his short, fat thighs. Eyes half closed, he was listening to the guard's voice on the public address system intoning the names of the various stations. Always the same voice. Ito-san had never felt any curiosity about the face behind the voice. That voice which not only gave the names of successive stations but listed all the possible connections, warned him not to leave anything behind him, cautioned him to take care getting off, etc. etc. It was all so reassuring. Ito-san heaved a grunting sigh of satisfaction and, pulling his jacket together, settled more comfortably on the bench that was warming his bottom.

The cup of green tea was steaming gently in front of him, slightly to the right, within reach of his hand. Bent over a sheet of white paper, Ito-san gave the impression of being plunged in deep concentration. His colleagues were not taken in by this. They themselves often adopted the same procedure in order to prolong their little morning nap. And yet, that morning, Ito-san was not sleeping. On the contrary, he had never felt more awake. His mind was in a state of excitement he had never known before. Although his face remained impassive, a host of passionate thoughts were jostling within the brain that was usually so serene. The delicacy of a hand with tapering fingers, a smile full of innocence and youthful promise, had been sufficient to upset the wonderful equilibrium characterizing Ito-san's life until then.

Ito-san had never been really interested in women. As a young man he had very soon been discouraged by the reactions of those little beings whose changing moods one could neither predict nor understand. The less he had to do with them, the better, he felt. Even at the university, the girls and the boys did not mingle, or only rarely. There was no female member of the FOB. His wife had simply been the necessary element in the perfect equilibrium of his life, but he had never given any thought to her as a woman. Was she pretty? He had never asked himself that question. In any case, on his mother's advice, he had always distrusted pretty faces. He had only to look around him to see the havoc such faces wrought. Passions, problems, torments. . . . He had always been a little afraid of them and had found it more practical to neutralize their influence upon his life. He had thus eliminated from his field of perception a certain number of things that threatened to disturb him. But this morning that psychological barrier had been rudely attacked, broken, annihilated, reduced to dust. Ito-san, his eyes still closed, had become a victim of passion. A mere look, a mere gesture was all that was needed to throw into confusion such a well-regulated existence. . . .

Mariko was one of those trainees who arrived every springtime to adorn the austere offices of the company. These young ladies fresh from university spent two or three years in a job before getting married. Their job was to serve tea several times a day to grumpy old men who always seemed preoccupied with something. They flirted nicely with the younger employees. They kept moving from one end of the building to the other, solemnly conveying notices explaining the explanation that would be explained during the meeting proposed for the next day. Above all, they kept smiling, and it was this smile that made their presence indispensable. Ito-san had seen hundreds of these young blossoms passing through the company. He had given all of them his blank look, which made them respect him deeply. Never had he allowed any pernicious day-dream to cross the desert of his emotional landscape. Never had he deigned to show the slightest interest in any of these temptresses. Never until this morning, a morning like any other, like so many other spring mornings. She had done no more than hand him his favourite cup of steaming green tea, greeting him with 'Ohayo gozaimasu, butcho-san.'[1] Ito-san's heart had sud-

---

[1] 'Ohayo gozaimasu' means 'Good morning', while 'butcho' is the equivalent of section chief. So 'butcho-san' means 'Mr Section Chief'. 'Satcho' (President), 'butcho', etc., become, as it were, family names used when addressing the person in question.

denly turned over, without warning, without his consent. His cheeks had very nearly started to colour. How awful! All Ito-san could do was to grab a sheet of paper and lower his head over it. Certain that his colleagues had not noticed his confusion, Ito-san endeavoured to get his body under control. But in reality he was simply trying to resist the temptation to raise his head and see what she was doing, to glimpse that look again, that grace. Slightly opening his eyes, without raising his head, he put out his hand to the cup in front of him. His hand was not trembling. He lifted the cup to his lips and noisily sucked in a mouthful of hot tea, which burnt his tongue. The familiarity of this gesture repeated so many times reassured him and he sat back in his chair as he put the cup back on his desk.

Suddenly Ito-san saw his life as a long succession of events without any importance, a chain of habits and conditioned reflexes. His whole life passed before his closed eyes and he saw in it nothing but boredom, boredom and still more boredom. In a flash, he understood the uselessness of his existence. He understood that he had spent his life rejecting all that would have given it value. For the first time, Ito-san was in love. For the first time, Ito-san was allowing emotions to get the upper hand of reason. He felt like a house that has been shut up too long, invaded all of a sudden by a beam of sunlight, the song of birds, the scent of flowers.

Ito-san suddenly realized that he had disregarded the source of his disquiet, the young girl who had handed him the cup of tea. He had allowed himself to be overwhelmed by the strong emotion she had provoked, but now his mind was turned towards that creature who had aroused him from his heavy slumber. He raised his head and inspected the familiar décor of the office surrounding him.

Watanabe-san, at the desk next to his, was busy meticulously sharpening his pencils one by one. He then arranged them in front of him after testing the sharpness of each point with his fingertip. A little further off, Yamamoto-san was talking into the telephone, all the while ducking his head in little bows and continually smiling at his invisible interlocutor. Uchida-san was engaged in affixing his personal seal to letters, one after the other. Standing in front of him, bent slightly forward in an attentive pose, there she was. Her eyes were fixed on Uchida's hand as if her life depended on that little white wood seal. Ito-san ventured to look her over. She must be twenty-two or twenty-three at the most. Her medium-length hair fell dead straight on the shoulders of her white blouse, but was waved in front and swept up on either side of her head in two charming little horns. He could see her face in profile. Her slightly lowered eyelids were fringed with long eyelashes. Her nose, a trifle long, was slender and straight except for the bridge where a slight bump lent it a touch of individuality. Her well-formed, sensual mouth sent a faint shiver running up and down Ito-san's spine. Under the shapeless white blouse that was standard wear for women employees of the company one could merely make out a figure which was slim but at the same time well rounded. Her bent arm was clasping a folder to her breast. Delicate wrist, hand of a milky whiteness, tapering fingers. On her feet the standard high-soled slippers that were part of the outfit of a female office worker. Dark stockings, almost black. Ito-san was grateful to her for not wearing those bobby socks which, he now realized, looked so ugly on a girl's legs. She leant forward to take the sheets of paper Uchida-san was holding out to her, and as she bowed her thanks she suddenly turned round. Her eyes met Ito-san's directly, as if she had always known he was watching her. But she lowered her eyes as soon as she saw Ito-san blush to the roots of his hair.

It was Ito-san's custom at midday to lunch on a *bento* composed of rice and a piece of cold fish or meat, left-overs from the evening meal. Every morning his wife, after helping him on with his overcoat, gave him the little rectangular box, divided into compartments, in which she had put the rice on one side, the little piece of fish or meat and pickled vegetables on the other. Ito-san, his attaché case on his desk, was gazing at the little box wrapped in a square of printed cloth. As he closed his attaché case upon it, he realized that he had never taken a more important decision in all his life. He stood up and joined Uchida and Watanabe who were already moving towards the door. When he asked them if he could join them for lunch, they both answered that they would be very happy, but their eyes could not conceal the astonishment they felt. Ito usually ate at his desk and spent the rest of the hour's break napping, lying back in his chair. They all three took the elevator to the basement, where there was a little restaurant which served noodle or rice dishes topped with meat, fish or vegetables. Ito-san's colleagues were in the habit of lunching there and when the three men entered the room they were greeted with cries of welcome from the restaurant staff, and from several tables came greetings from colleagues already seated there. Until now, Ito-san had had a horror of this kind of setting in which familiar and disagreeable smells of cooking and beer were mingled with bursts of laughter, arguments and the clash of crockery. But today, though outwardly impassive, he would have liked to have music, songs and dancing. He would have liked to drink sake. Alcohol at lunch – impossible! The three men spotted a little table vacant in a corner and went and sat down at it. Ito took a seat in the corner, his back to the wall, and grabbed the menu. Although that was what he had come there for, his heart gave a sudden bound when his eyes encountered those of Hiwatashi Mariko – he had discreetly checked the names of the new trainees in the office register. She was sitting with five or six other white-bloused young girls a few tables away from his own. He could hear the group's gurgles of laughter. Mariko was smiling, too, as she joined in the conversation, but Ito-san had the strange feeling that although her eyes had at once turned away from his, they were still looking at him.

Ito-san bought his newspaper and received his daily grunt of thanks, but for the last few days these everyday little events no longer had any importance. Ito-san took part in them even more mechanically than he had before, because his mind was now permanently occupied by the object of his desire. He kept seeing and assessing the slightest gestures, looks, words that had any kind of connection with Mariko. His colleagues had certainly noticed a change in his attitude but were far from attributing it to love. The first time he had gone down to lunch with them, they had thought he was going to announce some promotion for them or some modification in the running of the company. They had waited in vain for some declaration from him and had looked at one another questioningly when, after the meal was finished, they all got up to return to the office. Apart from looking a little more detached than usual, Ito-san had betrayed nothing to justify such a sudden disruption of routine. How stupefied they had been when next day at the same time Ito-san had accompanied them to the elevator. Ito-san could no longer do without Mariko's presence. His whole life was now nothing but a yearning to be in her presence again. Therefore he systematically threw away the contents of his *bento* box in the station toilets' trash-boxes. His wife would never have understood how, all of a sudden, he had become so capricious as to prefer meals in the uproar of a smoky little restaurant to the *bentos* arranged with her own hands.

Ito-san had not addressed a word other than 'thank you' to Mariko. No glance had really been exchanged except by accident. He had not yet thought of doing anything whatsoever to change this situation which was already acquiring an intensity he had never known before. It had still not occurred to him that he might be able to speak to her, to ask her what she thought of him. So when, one evening, he found himself alone in the elevator with Mariko standing there smiling in front of him, it was she who asked him if he was going straight home after work. An automatic reflex prompted him to reply 'Yes' before he realized, but too late, that he should have said 'No' and invited her to come and have a coffee with him. But, as if in an enchanted dream, he heard her gentle, clear little voice sounding above the buzzing in his ears and explaining to him that she preferred to wait in a certain tea-room until after the rush-hour. Hardly aware that it was he who was speaking, he heard himself saying that this evening he too would prefer to avoid the crowds and join her. Her only response was to look straight into his eyes and smile, which had the effect of making him lower them at once. By some miracle, the automatic doors opened on a dozen or so anonymous faces, and they left the elevator together.

With a cup of steaming tea in front of him, exactly as it had been a few weeks before when Mariko had put his cup on his desk for the first time, Ito-san underwent a metamorphosis. Everything had taken on a new fragrance. The blue of the sky, the green of the trees, the cotton-wool clouds. He now looked around him pityingly. Other people were bored to death, swamped by boredom, all those people who had never had the good luck to meet a Mariko. How he pitied them! He could not remember what his existence had been like previously without a little shiver of fear: he could have stayed buried alive without ever breathing the perfume of life! How had he been able to endure that condition for so many long years? His external appearance had certainly not altered. His face even seemed still more closed, hermetically closed. It was absolutely essential to keep up appearances. Ito-san knew that his peace of mind depended upon it. Therefore, apart from a few bizarre reactions they put down to overwork, his colleagues and his wife had noticed nothing. But Ito-san's interior life, of a dazzling whiteness, all sunbeams and flashing crystal prisms, was now all rejoicing, happiness, felicity. Yet there was one problem: by contrast, his daily surroundings appeared to him even more grey and dull, people's faces more bloodless and despairing. His wife had accepted the increase in overtime as the sign of a future promotion. How in any case could she have understood what was happening? If someone had gone to her and revealed the whole affair from A to Z with supporting evidence she still would have been incapable of believing it. Her husband's character simply did not fit the situation.

Meanwhile Mariko had been installed in a little apartment two underground train stops from her place of work. She had also intended to leave her parents' house in a distant Tokyo suburb, in order to live closer to the office. When things began to happen with Ito-san, it was decided that the latter would share the rent, contributing the equivalent of the amount he spent several times a week on 'love hotels' during after-office hours. So Ito-san paid half the rent and the service charges, allowing Mariko to find a comfortable apartment, two rooms and a private bathroom. Ito-san had simply had to ask his superior that his recent monthly salary increase should not appear on his salary sheet. This practice was very common among almost all the employees, to give them a little more pocket-money in addition to the pittance doled out by the wives to their worker-ant husbands, so the procedure aroused no suspicions. Mariko very soon turned the little two-room apartment into a perfect love-nest to which Ito-san flew as soon as an opportunity presented itself. She had bought him magnificent house slippers on which was embroidered the signature of a celebrated Parisian couturier, which could also be read on the bath towels. After his bath Ito-san would slip into a *yukata*[2] with a navy-blue pattern on a white ground and sit at the little low table of the living-room to sip his chilled beer and listen to the sweet chirruping of the young girl's chatter. Everything became delightful to hear, interesting to listen to. Even watching television took on a new dimension. When the couple lay down on the futon placed on the tatami, for Ito-san it was a time of forgetting and relaxation. The contact of that young and supple flesh, that vigorous yet gentle body. That love of life – a joy to be seized at every moment. Ito-san discovered sensuality and threw himself into it, wallowed in it with joyful abandon. When he arose from his amorous battles with Mariko, sucked dry but overcome with gratitude, he felt so alive, so here-and-now.

One day he ventured to ask Mariko why – why had she taken an interest in someone as devoid of fantasy as he? Her reply, though evasive, gave him to understand that it was precisely that austerity which had attracted her, that unshakeable demeanour, that hermetic appearance. She had experienced a totally feminine pleasure in breaking

---

[2] *Yukata*: a light cotton summer kimono, worn after the bath.

that carapace, in demolishing one by one the barriers protecting so jealously the emotions of this social monument that was Ito-san. And how grateful he was to her for it! Sometimes, in the train, he would start observing all those phantoms, nodding, their heads down on their chests or suspended from their strap-hangers' rings like puppets rocked by the movements of the carriage. Although his face remained quite impassive, he felt he wanted to shout at them to wake up, to open themselves to life. Life – was there anything more beautiful than life? What riches were worth more than life? What advanced technology deserved the sacrifice of a single life? To live – not just to subsist, not just to consume, not just to arrange an unimpeded passage through the allotted span given to every man on earth. Ito-san no longer wanted to see butterflies pinned on a bit of black cardboard. He wanted to see them fluttering against the blue of the heavens or the green of the grass. He wanted to see them disappearing behind a blossoming branch, then reappearing a few trees further on. He wanted a life in movement, a living life. Ito-san went home only in order to await the next day.

After a year and a half of this double existence Ito-san felt no fatigue or lassitude. On the contrary, he felt rejuvenated. Mariko was more and more adorable. He gave her little presents now and then, purchased with money taken from his salary before he handed it over to his wife. The latter was surprised by the lack of increases and the cuts in bonuses. But Ito-san had mentioned already several times, as if his thoughts were preoccupied by it, that the economic situation was not what it ought to be, and that small and medium enterprises were the first to suffer from it. In any case the house was paid for. True, there were monthly payments due on the superb four-door limousine that was parked in front of the house most of the time, and for the Empire-style dining suite that occupied all the available space in the little room, but these represented only half his salary. This left enough for the family's food and clothing requirements. No, the situation did not seem to be causing any problem. Ito-san was happy as he had never been before. Three evenings a week, on Mondays, Wednesdays and Fridays, he would take the last train home. From time to time, for appearance' sake, he gave his wife a few details about the work he was having to do or about the *nomiya*[3] where he had had to accompany his colleagues. But as a general rule his wife asked no questions and saw nothing inconvenient in these arrangements of their life, since her neighbours and the heroines of the soap operas she watched on television lived the same kind of life. It was this way of thinking that had resulted in the purchase of the latest model Toyota and the Empire dining-room suite. His wife too was happy in her own way. As for the children, they did not need him, he thought, and he did not need them.

Life was a permanent garden of roses for Ito-san. One Tuesday in November he was busy drawing up a report and trying to recollect in his imagination the marvellous contours of Mariko's beloved body through the white blouse when the internal telephone rang. Ito-san picked up the receiver, gave his name mechanically but sat up straight when he heard the voice of his boss. He was inviting him to have a drink with several colleagues after work. Ito-san knew that might be an occasion for his boss to make an important announcement, or simply to check up on his loyalty to the company. In the handbook of the perfect

[3] *Nomiya*: traditional popular eating-place where groups of company employees meet to get drunk and talk shop.

office worker there could be found in letters of gold: 'Thou shalt always be ready to go and get drunk with your colleagues on any evening whatsoever of the week.' Before Mariko, he had never had to complain about this kind of activity, which was part of the job. In those days, Ito-san asked no questions. Now, these outings took it out of him. What boredom there was in these male get-togethers in which they were sometimes joined by over-playful, over-made-up, over-professional hostesses. All such evenings had to end with popular songs massacred by each member of the group taking turns to stagger to the microphone, face aglow with sake, performing to the *karaoke*[4] accompaniment. . . . Then there was the stumbling walk of these men, wavering and staggering towards the last train that bore away its load of snoring, collapsing, giggling wrecks. Ito-san now knew that that was not what he could call pleasure. Suddenly he was struck by a suspicious thought. Why such an invitation at the last minute? Had the others noticed something? Had his work been suffering? The very thought that his boss was inviting him for a drink in order to warn him to watch his step gave him a cold sweat. What an insult that would be!

After taking its usual course, the evening was now well advanced. At the beginning the employees sat in fixed, stiff poses. The boss's attitude aimed at appearing relaxed and open, and this caused even greater embarrassment among

---

[4] *Karaoke*: recorded orchestral accompaniment for singers, minus voice. This kind of amateur singsong has become immensely popular not only in Japan but all over the world, wherever a few Japanese are gathered together.

the others. Now Ito-san could not help seeing how ridiculous these men were, their black-stockinged feet neatly tucked in under their bottoms as they knelt with hands on thighs, with head, eyes and smile attentive to the words of their superior. Their brilliant neckties were of natural silk. Then the old serving-maid brought in the beers and the bottles of hot sake. Everyone raised his glass and drank to the health of the company. From that moment the evening took on a different complexion. Just like the participants who, after two or three drinks, began to exhibit uniformly scarlet faces. Their postures had relaxed, the 'geisha' attitude, so attentive, had given way to the mettlesome and bantering 'samurai' persona. Seated cross-legged now, jackets removed and placed behind them on the tatami, but neckties still on duty, the men were calling out from one end of the low table to the other seeking confirmation from colleagues of this or that office anecdote or golfing episode. Ito-san, despite his dislike of such affairs, entered into the spirit and drank more than he should have. He was still waiting for his boss to intervene, for his presentiments had been confirmed by the furtive looks he had noticed being exchanged ever since the start of the evening. He seized one of the little bottles of sake and moved in a crouching walk to kneel slightly behind his boss who at once turned towards him, still laughing at a joke a young newcomer had just made in an effort to appear witty.

'Ito-san, dōmo!'[5] said the boss, holding out his tiny sake cup. Ito-san filled it to the brim, then his superior seized the bottle to fill in turn Ito-san's cup. The two men looked each other straight in the eye, a smile on their lips. Touching their minuscule cups, they wished one another 'Kampai!'[6] His boss seemed to be studying Ito-san's face;

---

[5] Dōmo: thank you. [6] Kampai!: Good health!

the rest of the group's attention was engaged in listening to an account of a wild evening when the new recruit had drunk so much sake that he had fallen asleep in a park, lying flat on his back on the gravel, arms outstretched, his attaché case still clutched in one hand. . . . Suzuki-san, still looking into Ito-san's eyes and smiling at him, began finally to talk. Ito-san's heart was beating twenty to the dozen but his smile too remained no less fixed. 'Ito-san, you seem to be in good form! I wanted to talk to you this evening about something which, while not official, is very close to my heart.' Ito-san's face, still impassive, became even more attentive. 'Fuji-san is going to be promoted managing director of the Osaka office. Takeuchi will have to go to replace poor Abe-san who has been the victim of that terrible accident. Takeuchi should have taken over Fuji-san's post. The President has telephoned me personally to ask if I thought you would be able to take it on. Before giving my final answer, I wanted to speak to you about it man to man. I know that it's an unprecedented approach, but then the situation also is unprecedented. . . .'

Ito-san's face was now of a copper-red colour, his ears felt hot, he regretted having drunk so much sake. His boss was quite simply telling him that he would probably be earning a double promotion. Fuji-san had a spacious private office with large bay windows overlooking the immense panorama of Tokyo. On the eighteenth floor, the penultimate one. Above, only heaven and the commander-in-chief: that was the source of all felicity. Fuji-san was Suzuki-san's right arm, and Suzuki-san was the right arm of the President himself. Fuji-san had a personal secretary and a black limousine at his disposal. Suzuki-san was looking at Ito-san. He was trying to get a glimpse of the conflicts, the mental upheaval, the panic perhaps behind that imperturbable mask. But Ito-san, eyes half closed, as nearly always, seemed to be lost in profound thought.

Eventually he began to speak, and uttered words that are proper in such circumstances. His voice was calm and steady. The tone of voice had so perfectly preserved that of a normal conversation that the others, even if they had noticed something was going on, were far from suspecting the importance of the dialogue. Finally Suzuki-san said, leaning slightly forward: 'If I have understood you correctly, you accept this responsibility. . . .' Ito-san without hesitating replied with a categorical affirmative.

The evening had passed as expected. Songs, more and more frequent rounds of drinks. Sake, then beer, then whisky and water, then sake again, then a bottle of French wine.

They moved on to another establishment, where the same procedure was followed. One eats something, fried fish, grilled chicken or baked potatoes or whatever. After a while it no longer has any importance. One gets up from time to time to go and bawl into a mike against a background of syrupy music. Then of one accord all set off for the station, a difficult, wavering and jovial procession. A little too jovial. For example, Ito-san is supporting Watanabe-san who, slumped on his shoulder, is pouring out long strings of friendly nothings, declarations of eternal fidelity. Tomorrow he will remember, or will choose to remember, nothing. Thus they can take up normal relations again unaffected by any embarrassment. All accompanied the boss to his train platform. Jovial, drunk as a pig, he nevertheless kept his dignity. Standing framed in the automatic doors, he saluted his team, who in a straight line on the platform were doubled up in deep bows which as they were repeated again and again became ever more risky. Eyes shining, they wished him a safe journey home and begged him to take care. The other passengers gazed at the spectacle with sleepy eyes. In fact most of them were already asleep, some of them sprawling on the long benches. The last train leaving one of the main stations looks more like the wreck of the *Titanic* than a means of public transport for decent citizens. Those decent citizens whose progress one can follow all along the platforms by the dollops of vomit from over-indulgence in alcohol and noodles.

The doors slide shut, open again briefly to allow an arm to free itself. The train moves off. Final bows before the windows of the departing carriage. Now the group is without its chief, and after a short period of hesitation they wish each other good-night in a tone of voice that tries to sound hearty, and each departs in the direction of his own last train.

Ito-san found himself alone in one of the vast underground passages whose walls and ceilings were covered with little white shining tiles such as one finds in bathrooms or public lavatories. He went over in his head all the events of that evening. His steps took him towards the station exit. He must announce the great news to Mariko. She was not expecting him, for it was not one of her evenings for him, but he knew she would be at home. He would pay her a surprise visit; she would be the first to learn that he was about to go up two storeys and sit at the desk of the section chief. She would be so proud of him. Perhaps later he could take her on as his personal secretary. Henceforward everything was possible. These thoughts intoxicated him as much as the alcohol he had drunk in the course of the long evening. . . . The taxi stopped in front of the 'manshun' where Mariko had her little apartment.

Ito-san opened the door with his own latchkey, taking care to make as little noise as possible. He wanted to surprise Mariko and slide into the sweet warmth of her futon. To whisper the good news in her ear and to rejoice in the eyes heavy with sleep that she would turn upon him. Then she would jump on top of him to rain little kisses on his neck, which always unleashed voluptuous tremors in him. He switched on the light in the tiny hallway where one took off one's shoes to change into house slippers and he received something like a stunning blow to the stomach. Next to the little shoes neatly pointing towards the entrance, ready to set off again, were two filthy, tatty sneakers of the type young people like to wear nowadays. The laces were not undone but the heels, trodden down, showed that they had been slipped on like common flip-flops. The sole of the right shoe was visibly more worn on the outside, proving that the owner had poor deportment. With a shiver of disgust Ito-san imagined that whoever owned them must drag his feet when walking. His own slippers with HIS embroidered on them had disappeared.

In his stockinged feet he placed his right foot on the step up from the entrance and was immediately riveted to the spot, as if he had seen a rattlesnake. Against the sliding paper door to the living-room there lay the grotesque heap of a pair of stone-washed jeans. One of the legs was turned inside-out and the heavy buckle of the belt lay on the floor like an abandoned weapon. Mechanically Ito-san slid open the frame of the *shoji* – the door whose thin, opaque paper was stretched on little rectangles of fine wooden strips. In front of him he beheld a veritable battlefield. Dirty plates, a packet of biscuits, an ashtray overflowing with cigarette-ends covered the little low table. The square, flat cushions were arranged in two piles on which one could imagine two people sitting and eating, drinking, talking, laughing. Empty beer-cans here and there on the tatami. Three-quarters empty, a bottle of the cheapest kind of Japanese wine available stood on top of the television. The door to the bedroom was half open. The interior was dark. A black hole towards which Ito-san moved as if hypnotized. His eyes took some time to get used to the darkness. Gradually he began to make out a futon creating a pale patch on which two bodies were entangled. One of the bodies was partly covered with Ito-san's *yukata*. The chest thus revealed appeared sun-tanned and muscular, as did a long, bare thigh covered with black hairs. Ito-san felt a shiver run through him to the depths of his being. The body of Mariko now shone whitely in the semi-darkness like a jewel in a black velvet jewel-box. It was completely naked: her face was covered by her loosened hair. Ito-san did not move: he stood petrified by the spectacle before his eyes.

Mariko, sensing a presence in the room, opened her eyes. Behind the curtain of her hair she made out the square of light coming from the living-room, against which the plump form of Ito-san stood out like a shadow puppet. She could see his heavy bust surmounted by the massive head. The short arms hung down slightly away from the body. She caught sight of the attaché case Ito-san was still holding in his right hand. Although she could distinguish nothing of his features, Mariko could imagine Ito-san's face. She could visualize it all the more clearly in that she knew it was practically unchanged despite the utter stupefaction he must be feeling. At the very most, his little eyes must be blinking convulsively as they tended to do under the influence of great excitement. After a few minutes she sat up, leaning on her elbow, swept the hair away from her face and said in a sleepy voice: 'But it's Tuesday.' Ito-san had not budged an inch. She dragged towards her the dressing-gown that had been flung aside on the tatami, slipped it on as she was getting up, gently shoved Ito-san into the living-room and closed the door behind her. With automatic gestures she began to tidy the room. She had soon collected ashtrays, glasses and rubbish, which she carried to the sink. She switched on the electric kettle. In a twinkling she had put the floor cushions back in their respective places and the little room had regained its serious, respectable look. She turned towards Ito-san, who was still standing in the same position, his attaché case in his hand. His expression was set and expressionless. 'Sit down. We're going to drink a cup of tea.' As if in confirmation, the kettle began to chirrup. Ito-san placed his attaché case on the tatami, knelt on a cushion in a corner of the room and leant his shoulders against the wall, thus taking up the pose of a Buddha enshrined in the niche of a temple.

'He's wearing my *yukata*,' he managed to get out after a moment.

Mariko studied him closely, then, after giving a nod of understanding, got up, gathered the sleeper's things together, slid open the door, went in and slid it shut behind her. There were some growls from next door, then whispers. After a moment or two the sliding door was reopened. Mariko came out and again slid the door shut behind her. The urgent whistling of the kettle called her to the kitchen corner where she busied herself, making delicate little noises with the china. Finally she turned round, carrying a black lacquer tray on which steamed two magnificent teacups of the same pattern but different in size and colour. Mariko's was dainty, in pastel colours, while Ito-san's was bigger, thicker, coarser, in earth colours. Just as she was placing the tray between herself and Ito-san and was kneeling gracefully on the floor, the door slid open and Ito-san's *yukata* was tossed into the room with a soft thud. Ito-san and Mariko who had seen it at the same time turned their eyes away at once. Thirty seconds later a tall, slender young man with overlong hair and a deep tan entered the room. Ito-san felt ridiculous and helpless. Taking no notice of him, the young man said, using the customary Japanese formula, that he was sorry to be leaving before everyone else, and left the room.

One of his jeans pockets was coming unstitched and his white T-shirt bore on the back, in big red letters, some meaningless inscription in English. He could be heard getting into his sneakers in the hallway, then the front door closed and his dragging footsteps moved slowly away.

Silence returned to the room. Far away one could hear the ceaseless rumble of taxis patrolling the Tokyo night. An ambulance siren suddenly shrieked in the next street and made them jump. They looked at one another. The tea was still steaming between them. Neither of them had touched the cups. 'I'm going to take Fuji-san's place,' he announced in a dull, lugubrious voice. Mariko bent her head again, gazing fixedly at her hands resting on her thighs. A good ten minutes passed before Ito-san opened his mouth again to ask 'Why?'

At first, Mariko did not move, then, very slowly, she raised her head and looked Ito-san in the eyes. 'Because he is young and he's beautiful and I love him.' Ito-san, his voice now sounding hoarse, his face expressing total incomprehension, managed to bring out in a stifled cry: 'But you told me you loved *me*.'

'And I love you, I do. I love you both. You for certain things, him for others.' Mariko was silent then went on in a calm, steady voice: 'He wants to marry me.'

Ito-san gazed at her intently, hanging on her words.

'He's a photographer. He spends half the year travelling abroad. I've told him everything about us two, and he said he felt relieved to know you would be taking care of me during his absences. . . .'

One hand slung through one of the plastic rings hanging from the ceiling of the carriage, he was swaying to the movements of the train. In front of him a seat became vacant but he did not consider taking it. He was lost in thought. His life had taken a new turning. An unexpected turning. His present situation, a source of joy to his wife, had lent another dimension to his life. He was working even harder than before. Every evening he had to go out with clients. He came home only at weekends when he was not needed for games of golf or other activities with clients. Mariko had become his private secretary. She also took part in the various dinners and evening parties, in case Ito-san should need her services. They slept in luxury hotels in which the company had rooms permanently reserved for its top staff. His wife, her possible protests silenced by her husband's undreamt-of promotion, had in any case no cause to complain. She even took pride in deploring to her neighbours the fact that she was seeing less and less of her husband, which signified that he was becoming more and more indispensable to his company. It made her feel proud rather than disturbed. And she had so much to do looking after her children's education. She had entered her daughter, still more sullen and withdrawn, in a tea ceremony course in an attempt to instil the grace and femininity she lacked. She knew quite well that when the time came for her daughter to marry, the only solution would be the *omiai*.[7] As for the son, it was difficult to see where he had sprung from. His energy, his lust for life caused him to rebel against the regulations his school tried to force upon him. All he wanted was to play games, run, let himself go. He had a hard time accepting discipline. He could not understand why he had to memorize so many useless, senseless things when there were so many more interesting things to be discovered. Both children attended

[7] *Omiai*: arranged marriage.

a special school in the evenings and at weekends, in order to cram for their examinations.

Mariko had got married just after her appointment to the position of private secretary to Ito-san. The latter had accepted the situation more readily than she had expected. It even seemed to her that once the first shock was over he had felt a certain relief. In fact he had always feared that sooner or later she would leave him to get married.

Ito-san's life had regained its equilibrium. His passion for Mariko had been replaced by a sort of perfect contentment, a complete satisfaction, nirvana. As a company director, Ito-san had even attended the marriage of Mariko and Abe-san. In a black morning suit, with his look of a black, lacquered strong-box, he had made a superb impression in his address to the young couple. He had spoken as a boss praising the merits of his employee, but also as a father listing the thousand and one qualities of the daughter he was about to lose. The gathering of wedding guests, usually apathetic on such occasions, had appreciated the depth of Ito-san's sentiments. Only Abe-san's smile, a half-amused, half-sarcastic smile, had threatened to put him out of countenance.

He could not get used to Abe-san, to his nonchalance, his free-and-easy ways, the derisive smile he gave to everything. He hardly ever talked about his experiences in foreign lands, though one got the impression that he had had a lot of them. He watched people fussing around him as an adult watches children making ready for a game or preparing a birthday party. On the rare occasions when he had found himself in his presence, Ito-san had felt he was a superior being. Not at all like the superiority of his bosses: that was merely a hierarchical superiority, based on position in the company. But with Abe-san he always had the feeling he was confronted by someone whom nothing could touch. There was, of course, the ridiculous situation of having to share a woman. Ito-san had asked Mariko how Abe-san felt about it. For Abe-san, Mariko and Ito-san were indulging in an incestuous relationship, her boss being the father of the company. That had made Mariko laugh and Ito-san furious.

Abe-san made trips to far-off places all the year round, with regular stopovers in Tokyo where it seemed as if he returned only in order not to forget his roots, his culture, his contacts. He loved Mariko in his own way, the way in which he did everything – that is, as if the matter did not really concern him. He had told her that her little-girl behaviour refreshed him, because in his travels round the world he saw too many horrors that he could forget for a while whenever he returned to her infantile universe: too many evils in Japanese society also, but so devious and hidden from sight that they were never noticed by the public. Mariko declared that he was never angry when he made those criticisms, only a little weary sometimes. 'The Japanese don't know how to have a good time, and yet they are still little children' was the sort of phrase that often recurred in his conversation. Mariko drank in his words, which irritated Ito-san, but she refused to go all the way with Abe-san's ideas. He would say: 'Nothing bothers them as long as they can go on with their humdrum daily lives. . . . Famines, catastrophes, disasters and other world-shaking events do not interest them. They have no real compassion. And whenever they say "Kawaiso",[8] it's just a formula, a way of speaking. . . .' Sometimes he infuriated Mariko with such comments, whose injustice she denounced. Then he would smile, drawing her to him: 'You're right! You mustn't listen to my foolish talk.' In fact

[8] Kawaiso: What a shame! What a pity!

he rarely allowed himself to express his intimate thoughts in this way. Usually he strove to avoid all serious discussions. When Mariko had asked him why, he had started to reply with 'When in Rome. . . .'

Abe-san had left for three months in the United States. Ito-san was getting to look more and more like those politicians one sees leaving big limousines and trotting, small but dignified, between two ranks of journalists and press photographers of whom they haughtily take no notice. His suit was more navy blue than ever, the parting in his hair straighter than ever, the corners of his mouth more turned down than ever. Everything in his appearance fitted the correct image of an incorruptible and untouchable company official. Even Mariko would sometimes forget that it was the same man whom at intimate moments she would call 'My big baby'. She did not tell him it was a phrase used by Abe-san. Whenever he was in Tokyo, he had told her one day, in the train, he felt as if he were surrounded by a lot of big babies looking for their mammies.

Mariko was looking at the beautiful air-mail envelope torn down one edge. The stamp and the foreign cancellation mark lent it an exotic air. The two sheets of paper of a dazzling whiteness stood out against the mottled brown top of the low table. She gazed without reading them at the little Chinese characters written by Abe-san on the letter paper. The cup of coffee she had made for herself to drink while reading the letter, thus giving herself double pleasure, had grown cold and a thin, brownish, rubbery skin had formed on the surface.

With the first words of the letter, Mariko had sensed catastrophe. The label EXPRESS in red letters had not aroused any suspicion. Abe-san often wrote by express air mail. This time his news fully deserved such urgency. Abe-san could not telephone her from the remote outpost in the Borneo jungle where he was at present. He had dismissed the possibility of sending a telegram as too impersonal. And yet the matter was of the utmost urgency. Following an acute attack of viral hepatitis, Abe-san had had to submit to a blood test to make sure there were no dangerous viruses now present in his system. The analysis had produced no results on that count. Everything had returned to normal. Yet traces of an odious disease had been discovered. After many more tests, the verdict was given: Abe-san had been contaminated. This disease was highly contagious. Mariko and Ito-san would both have to undergo a blood test as soon as possible. Abe-san gave the addresses of three Tokyo clinics where the necessary analyses could be performed. Mariko just could not get to grips with the situation. It had been a brutal shock. The consequences could be dramatic. A tear glistened at the corner of her right eye. A nightmare, a bad dream, that's all it was – it could only be a nightmare. The telephone rang. With a mechanical gesture she took up the receiver. It was from the office, where they were surprised she had not come in that morning. Was everything all right?

'You are indeed Mr Ito?' The little man with the tortoise neck had spoken in an alarmingly loud yet shrill voice. In two armchairs facing the desk, two younger men were seated: he had just noticed them. They had turned round and looked in his direction, over their shoulders. One over his right shoulder, the other over his left shoulder. Ito-san examines their faces, one after the other. In their eyes, he can read curiosity, surprise, interest, contempt. . . .

Ito-san becomes the first case of Aids reported in Japan.

She Was So Pretty

High school was where the hell really started. M. was just fourteen years old, a living picture of youth and beauty.

Despite all her attempts to be as inconspicuous as possible, as soon as she came near the boys, they became more noisy, more boisterous, trying to attract her attention. They never looked really straight at her, but it seemed as if their eyes were always upon her. She had the distinct feeling that whenever they started kicking up a racket near her, everything they did, said, was for her sake alone.

Unfortunately others noticed this state of affairs, and one day after school as she was walking to the station, her life was completely overturned.

She was walking with eyes lowered. Suddenly she sensed a presence on either side of her. At first she just glimpsed two unusually long gym dresses and her heart began to beat wildly. The pleated blue-serge dresses hung down lower than the calf. M. knew all too well the meaning of this vestimentary detail. The girls were high-school 'gangsters'. If they started taking an interest in some unfortunate girl for one reason or another, it was to torment and threaten her until the latter agreed to do everything they demanded of her. Mostly that meant handing over her pocket-money. But it could also mean accompanying them to Shinjuku or Shibuya[9] to carry their school bags while they made the acquaintance of boys with long, greasy hair dressed in Elvis Presley style, and wearing school uniform jackets reaching sometimes to below their knees. These were the male versions of the girl gangsters. The 'chiefs', the little bosses, detestable, wicked types, who in their turn had their own following of poor little frightened boys carrying the chiefs' school bags. The 'slaves' waited on their masters until the latter were so good as to allow them to go home and do their homework, while their chiefs squandered the boys' pocket-money on Coca-Cola and cigarettes.

M. knew this problem and always avoided any confrontation with these young, slave-driving girls. Their choice always fell upon the most timid, or on those who were most different from the norm. One could fall into disgrace with them for various reasons: too fat, too tall, too short, too timid, too reserved, too anything. The fact of being even slightly different for one reason or another was sufficient to attract the attentions of these torturers, who then would vent all their fury on their victims. M. had already witnessed some of these persecutions but had always, like the rest of her schoolmates, avoided getting involved with them, pretending not to see anything. Sometimes she had a guilty feeling for not extending a helping hand to these wretched victims, but to have done so would have meant throwing herself into the lions' den and laying herself open to the same torments as those

[9] Shinjuku and Shibuya are lively shopping and entertainment districts of Tokyo, popular with the young.

suffered by the unfortunate boy or girl with whom she sympathized. One could see him or her growing more wretched day by day. A girl who at first was by nature happy and open-hearted lost all joy in life from one day to the next: it could be seen in her eyes. She would skip school more and more often. Her work and her marks became deplorably bad. Everybody, the teachers, the pupils, noticed it. Everybody knew quite well what the cause was. And nobody did anything about it.

So M. found herself being accompanied by these two navy-blue dresses that were too long. Eyes lowered, she did not even try to hurry away from them. She was waiting. The two girls walked beside her like that for two or three hundred yards without saying anything, one on each side of her. Suddenly the girl on her left began to speak. She was addressing the other girl. She said with exaggerated vulgarity, using a rough, crudely bantering tone and the vocabulary of young toughs: 'You're right, you know, she really is a nice little bit of stuff.' She went on: 'Take a good look at those plump lips of hers and those long lashes.' The other continued: 'And those long legs, she must have American blood in her, the little bastard, she can't be a real Japanese.'

The language, the cruel words had already almost made M. break down and sob. Yet she continued on her way like a sleepwalker. The street leading to the little suburban station seemed never-ending. She could still hear the same familiar noises, the shouts of the vegetable woman praising the quality of her strawberries, the thousandfold jinglings of the little steel ball-bearings in the pachinko parlour, the screech of bicycle brakes passing close to her.

As well as the familiar street sounds, there was the deafening beat of M.'s heart within her breast and, outside, the snarling voices of the two tormentors. That first day they did no more than accompany her to the entrance of the station. They stopped in front of the ticket-puncher and shouted after her: 'Bye-bye, see you tomorrow!' Two high-school girls seeing their friend off at the station. . . .

Once the train doors had closed, M. took a deep breath and began to consider what sort of life she was going to have from now on.

Next day, as she expected, they were there waiting for her at the school gates. As soon as they caught sight of her, they went to meet her, smiles on their faces, again just like two school friends greeting a third: 'Well now, darling, you look tired this morning, you haven't slept well, you're not pleased to see us, you'd rather it were Jun Kun coming to meet you. You're quite stuck on Jun, aren't you, you little minx!!!'

Jun was the idol of girls like these. His success derived from his supposed resemblance to a *talento*, a popular television singer. Actually this resemblance was mainly based on the special care he took to imitate his model's hair-style. Jun must have noticed M., and that alone was sufficient to unleash the resentment of these little 'boss girls'.

In any case, by the very fact of her astonishing beauty, M. stood out from the group, therefore drawing down upon herself the terrors of *ijime*.[10] Persecutions were generally the result of some physical peculiarity, but in Japanese society, where everyone tried to look the same and not stand out from the group, this 'charming' quality was much admired, this kind of stupidly childlike or infantile look adopted by adults, these rather soft features that formed a fairly agreeable expression – yes, it was tolerated, this silly-young-girl type that was imitated by women

[10] *Ijime*: bullying.

from sixteen to twenty-six and even older. On the other hand, there was less tolerance for outright beauty whose very extraordinariness was found disturbing. M. was to be bullied for being too beautiful.

The days went by, each one bringing its share of tortures and frustrations. As soon as they noticed that M. had become the current victim, her best friends began to avoid her.

On the first day, Yumiko, seeing her flanked by the two other girls, had come to greet her as usual, but had not been able to stop herself blushing slightly. She had talked only in the most banal and impersonal way. M. had sensed that her friend's mind was already engaged in calculating the extent of the danger in being seen with her and thinking of the best way to avoid being trapped in the same difficult situation.

Soon M. found herself more and more isolated until she had no contact with anyone. Only her tormentors were always on hand. Her life became a daily hell on earth; when she was not being humiliated, ill-treated or insulted, she counted the moments until her agony would begin again. She was too timid to talk about it with her teachers. In any case, she had formed the distinct impression that they had well and truly noticed what was happening but that they had not dared make a move. All too often they turned their eyes away at the sight of the trio. They could not help seeing M. carrying the school bags of her two 'mistresses', in addition to her own, from one class to another.

At first, despite her natural timidity, M. tried to rebel. One morning, for example, during the break between the history lesson and the English class, she refused to go and buy for them their favourite cakes stuffed with red bean paste which a shopkeeper always kept warm on a hotplate in front of her stall.

'Ooh! I suddenly feel hungry! You'd better go and buy us a couple of cakes during the next break.' Five minutes. That meant running right at the end of the history class, sneaking past the gatekeeper (as it was forbidden to leave the premises during school hours), running the five hundred yards separating the school from the station, buying the cakes with the money they had kindly allowed her to keep; then running all the way back as fast as possible, passing through the gate again, arriving late, sweating and breathless, for the English class with the two little hot cakes. What humiliation!

M. had lowered her eyes and said 'No'.

'What?' the bigger of the two girls had squawked. 'What's that you said?'

'No. I won't go,' M. had repeated in ever-weaker tones.

They had thereupon burst into horrifying laughter, as if M.'s refusal had pleased them. 'We'll see about that after history. . . .'

They had gone into the history class. A whole hour of it. . . . M.'s heart kept beating wildly all through it. Eyes lowered to her book, she did not dare look up for fear of encountering the others' cruel smiles.

End of class. At once, the two navy-blue dresses were on either side of her desk.

'Come on, get a move on.'

As if in a nightmare she had stood up. As in a nightmare she found herself in the toilets, on her knees on the wet floor. One of the pair was twisting her arm behind her back, the other was gripping the back of her neck with all her strength and pushing her face down. The flood of water arrived with a noise like thunder, wetting her face and hair hanging down on either side. Her stomach heaved and she felt she was going to vomit as the water was forced through her nostrils and trickled down the back of her throat, making her feel she was drowning. At the end of thirty interminable seconds, they relaxed their grip and ran away cackling, shouting insults and threats at her.

On her drenched face tears were rolling. Leaning back now against the greyish wall, she wept. She felt humiliated, broken, dirty – as dirty as the odour she breathed through all her pores. Her navy-blue gym dress was stained and rumpled, her white bobby socks marked with disgusting brown streaks. She stood up, sobbing her heart out. Her neck and her arm hurt her a great deal. She gazed at herself for a long time in the mirror.

Even in this pitiful state she was magnificent, perhaps even more beautiful than usual. The hair stuck to her face, her eyes swimming with tears lent her a wild and desperate appearance. She was beautiful, and yet the sight filled her with horror.

That day M. went and notified the school office that she was not feeling well, and returned home early.

There was no one at home. Her mother must have gone with her friends to a tea-room on the Ginza, one of those places where you did your utmost to forget that you were in Japan. One day her mother had taken her to a café where the young waiters passed on their orders in French. When the waiter had repeated their order in broken French, M. had not been able to stop herself giving a little laugh and she had given him a wide-eyed look.

She went upstairs, tidied her hair, put on her nightdress and went to bed. It was two o'clock in the afternoon.

A little before five she heard the key in the front door lock, high heels tapped two or three times on the tiles of the little entrance where shoes were removed. Then just afterwards, cautious steps.

M.'s mother had seen her shoes in the entrance and had gone upstairs at once. Just before reaching M.'s bedroom door, she had called softly 'M. . . .'

M. had drawn the curtains and the room was plunged in semi-darkness. After the brilliance of the light outside, her mother had difficulty adjusting to it. But slowly she began to make out the futon spread in the centre of the room's tatami floor. She and her husband had opted for the Western-style bedroom, throned by the double bed, leaving only a narrow space all round it. Among the confusion of covers and pillows her mother, feeling worried now, could see M.'s loosened hair. As was her custom, she was lying on her stomach.

Her mother approached the futon and sat down beside it on the tatami. She spoke to her softly: 'What's the matter? Are you sick? Did you take your temperature?'

Without changing her position, M. shook her head.

'Are you in any pain?'

Again M. shook her head.

Her mother stands up. M. hears her opening the small medicine chest in the bathroom. Then a sound of metallic or plastic objects knocking against each other. The medicine chest being shut. M. turns over. 'I'm not sick.'

Her mother is standing there framed in the doorway, in her stockinged feet, and behind her, just beyond the brown border of the tatami, her house slippers arranged with the toes neatly pointing outwards, like two well-trained little pets. She is holding a thermometer.

'Well then, what's wrong with you?'

M. begins crying softly, her face again buried in the pillows.

Her mother lets her cry like that for two or three minutes. She strokes her hair gently. Her face is worried.

Today M. did not go to her *juku*.[11] She heard her mother telephoning there from downstairs to apologize for her absence.

Lying on the futon, eyes gazing up at the ceiling, M. is day-dreaming about a life in which there would be no more school, no more having to be accountable to others, no more accounts to be given. A life in which she could walk anywhere without having to think how she should walk, speak without having to think how she should speak. A life in which she need no longer be afraid of being different, of being abnormal. When she watches foreign movies on television or at the cinema, she cannot help envying those young people in them who think only of amusing themselves, doing as they please, saying whatever comes into their heads. Over there, the more 'different' one is, the better! Of course, it's only a movie. . . . And one never hears much about the difficulties they may encounter in not being able to belong to a cosy, protective group. How lonely they must sometimes feel! Just as M. feels now. Alone, so alone. Her mother had been sweet and gentle. She had tried to understand, but in vain. She had even suggested going to see the teachers, to ask their advice. As if that could change anything. No, she hadn't a clue. Put into ordinary words, M.'s problem seems so ordinary, so childish! A crisis. No one can measure the extent of its seriousness, nor how much that kind of wounding hurts. She is all alone, and she knows it.

What can she do to endure it all? Will she be able to

---

[11] *Juku*: night school, considered indispensable if one wishes to cram for examinations. Even small children are forced to attend *juku* in order to pass entrance exams for junior school.

endure it? She raises herself on her elbow a little so as to see her reflection in the mirror of the doll's house dressing-table standing on the tatami. In the semi-darkness of her bedroom she has difficulty making out her features: her hair is a mess.

'Sexy.' Several boys have pronounced that word as she passed by.

'Sexy.' That English word sounded so vulgar, bizarre.

After two days' absence from the high school M. took up her cross again. A few of her schoolmates had come to ask after her health, it is true. But M. could sense their wish to be elsewhere, not to be seen in her company.

M., pestilential outcast, feels she is living and moving in a nightmare world. She acts like a mechanical doll, repeating gestures learnt long ago by heart. It is perfectly possible to exist like that. From the viewpoint of normal Japanese society, everything seems perfectly in order. The gestures, the attitudes, all are in order. The clockwork keeps functioning, so everything must be all right! No problem. Yet if they took the trouble to look at M., they would see that something inside the mechanism is out of order. In her eyes they would notice no spark of life. No life at all.

The two others at once started their little games again. M. no longer reacts. She has accepted her condition. They have won.

It is almost summer. The cold weather has completely vanished, making way for warm days followed by mild evenings, with a tepid but pleasant breeze. Soon it will be the rainy season. Soon there will come torrid, humid days. Soon the Tokyo air will become sticky, suffocating.

Suddenly M. is dreaming of snowy slopes, blue skies, dry, tonic air, purity. Her dream leads her to start thinking of death.

She is walking along walls covered with thousands of red flowers with a powerful, sweet scent. As she passes in front of the brown doorway to a small house, the dog, small and brown too, hurls itself forward on its chain, ridiculous in its fury. Every evening the same thing happens. At first M. had attempted to make friends with the creature, talking to it softly and putting her hand through the railings of the front gate, trying to stroke it. But these tentative approaches had made it only more hysterical. Now she simply looks at it sadly. She wonders if it does not remind her of lots of people she sees around her every day. Indeed, she wonders if it does not resemble her two torturers. Could they, too, be pulling on their chains? This thought arouses no compassion in M.'s heart, but rather a painful anger.

Today they had been particularly nasty.

Oh! she hates them so.

Life goes on. M. gets used to it. Already she can no longer remember a time when, as a good high-school pupil, her only worries were to keep up with the others in class, to keep her nose to the grindstone, to pass successfully the memorization tests, to give her parents, her teachers, everyone, just what was expected of her. Now, in addition to all those little problems, she carries within her a cancer that is eating her soul. But she becomes accustomed to it as one becomes accustomed to a long illness. All the frustrations inflicted upon her now form an integral part of her daily life. She has got used to never feeling any joy in living, any enthusiasm. She has got used to everything, but the sickness is still there deep inside her, and sometimes she suffers long bouts of depression.

It is in one of these depressive states that she begins to think of death. Then very soon she starts dreaming of her death, her very own death. The death lying in wait for her.

Gradually she begins fondling this idea of death, seeing in it the only possible deliverance from her wretched existence. Yes, her existence: what is she getting out of it, really? No more joys, no more pleasures either. Her life is nothing but a long succession of hours divided between study, the brutality of her two torturers, and waiting for. . . . Her death is the reward for that waiting, the end of fear, the end of the fear of fear, of pain. Her death will bring together all her friends or former friends, her parents. Her death will bring disgrace upon her two enemies. She begins to think of death as her only friend. Her only faithful friend, always there, wherever she goes, whatever she is doing.

So every time her life becomes too unbearable she takes refuge in that idea of death. Her mother gives her worried looks whenever she finds her smiling blissfully before an open book she is not reading or a television screen she is not watching. 'M.,' she often asks her, 'is everything all right? Are you feeling all right? Do you need anything?' She is unable to tell her she finds her bizarre. Sometimes M. makes her feel a little afraid.

How could she tell her she makes her feel a little afraid? So she says nothing. She watches her out of the corner of her eye. M. does not notice her watching her. Her mother does indeed feel something should be done, but she does not know what. She does not know how to communicate such unusual thoughts. M. cannot explain her agony to her: her mother does not know how to approach her. She has been taught all kinds of things, but not that. She has been taught the tea ceremony, how to run the home, raise her children, look after her husband, get on with the neighbours, her family, society. She has been taught the best ways to shop, to buy consumer goods, to organize her life and the life of her family. But no one has ever taught her how to come to the aid of her own daughter. No one has taught her how to help her daughter overcome her psychological distress. So she stands to one side, powerless and pitiful.

M. is preparing her suicide as one prepares a holiday trip. As soon as she has a free moment, she goes over again and again all the details of the place, the time. She has decided on the date, the 30th of JUNE. Why? She does not really know. It is in the rainy season, but M. hopes that on that evening it will not be raining. It would be best if it had just been raining and the whole city were shining after having been washed by one of those torrential cloudbursts. The moment had been revealed to her the day she had heard of the death of her favourite singer, I.A., who had jumped to her death from the top of a ten-storey building. For several days M. was thinking of using the same building, but eventually she decided that her place of death should be hers and hers alone.

So it was necessary to find her own building, in her own district – the district that was her favourite in Tokyo, Harajuku. She had chosen this place because of its great tree-bordered boulevard that made one think of Europe. Besides, some people actually called it 'The Champs-Elysées of Japan'. On this avenue a magnificent new building had just been completed. As in so many recent constructions, from the ground floor up one was in the lap of luxury. Right from the entrance it was all deep carpeting and chromium-plated steel, with immense mirrors. Salesgirls in the latest Paris fashions Elegant boutiques. Discreet background music. It was a place in which to spend money, but one also felt as if one were in a museum of modern art. The most celebrated couturiers had their boutiques there on every floor. They could be reached by a huge central spiral staircase. There was also an external elevator. One day, M. had taken the elevator to the top storey. The elevator girl had greeted her with a formal bow before beginning to rattle off her string of polite formula phrases and information on what the various floors had on offer for customers. All delivered in a falsely infantile and mechanical voice.

On the top floor, the ninth, there was an Italian restaurant giving on to an enormous hall. At the entrance a young lady behind a little counter, a very beautiful young lady. As soon as the automatic doors of the elevator opened with a pneumatic sigh, the woman behind her little counter had cried an elegant 'Irrashai-imasse'. This welcoming phrase was addressed especially at a couple the elevator had picked up some floors below – he very tall, very blond and very American, she very Japanese, looking very tiny next to him, with long jet-black hair hanging straight down her back.

The counter lady, after having rapidly weighed up the high-school uniform worn by M., had concentrated all her attention on the young couple. The girl had handed her her jacket. They had entered the restaurant. The hall was now almost empty. A young man wearing shoes with monstrously thick soles was smoking a cigarette on a sofa covered with brilliant white plastic material. Beside him a telephone, brilliant crimson, stood out against the pale wall.

M. had made her way towards the toilets, situated in a little corridor. There were doors facing one another on either side of the corridor. At the end, there could just be seen another door of the same colour as the walls, flushed perfectly with the surrounding wall and with a brass handle that could be lifted out of its recessed setting. M. seized hold of the handle and turned it. Without a sound the door opened a few inches. It was heavy, built of massive metal, but it gave way easily enough. The open air whipped at M.'s body after the air-conditioned calm of the interior. The bright light made her eyes blink. She pulled the door shut behind her, began to mount a stair. She found herself on a vast terrace. All around her there were houses, buildings as far as the eye could see. In the setting sun, Mount Fuji, resplendent, perfect, was standing there like a target, the focus for the immense city.

At that precise moment M.'s hesitations were swept away by the light breeze blowing on her face. No more doubts: she had to die.

M. took a deep, noisy breath. She realized she had been holding her breath ever since she had opened the door. The reprehensible nature of her action, the beauty of the setting, the atmosphere of the moment almost made her suffocate. For a good ten minutes she stood there, stuck in the middle of the immense terrace without being able to move. Living in Tokyo, she was not accustomed to having so much empty space for herself alone, in which her gaze could lose itself in the horizon. After a while she moved to one side and found herself confronted by a fence. A safety fence, against whom? Against what? Down below, jutting out from the next floor, she could see a cerulean-blue swimming-pool; M. could see only part of it but she could hear the voices of restaurant clients dining beside the pool, hidden from view by the overhang. A swimming-pool suspended in air in the middle of Tokyo. The image made the girl smile. She crossed the terrace. This side overlooked the avenue. The noise of traffic rose muted from below. At six o'clock in the evening the traffic was dense. The cars, bumper to bumper, formed a long, multi-coloured ribbon. They had the look of children's toys. Enclosing the broken ranks of metallic car bonnets, the green of the leafy trees created a rich, velvety effect. The perfect spot. The people walking under the trees were hidden from sight. Strangely enough, there was no safety fence on this side.

Tuesday, 13th June. On M.'s desk a letter. The paper is beautiful and her name is written with care, in the old style. The envelope has a black border. Before opening it M. sits awhile as if hypnotized by the *kanjis*[12] of her name. She sees her hands take the envelope, open one side, remove a beige-coloured page of the same kind of paper. M. is now reading her own obituary. In formal style they have inscribed her name, her address, her age and the announcement of her death.

Following the accepted formulae, there is a list of signatures. There are about thirty of them. At the top, naturally, come the names of her persecutors. Other names too, names of girls who had once been her friends. M. also recognizes the name of the history teacher. They must have meant it as a jest, a grisly joke! Despite her apathy, M. feels her stomach contract. Her eyes begin to glitter. In her distress she sees the faces of the two tormentors who have come to enjoy the effect they have produced. M. looks at her hands, which are trembling slightly. She puts the sheet back in the envelope which

---

[12] *Kanjis*: Chinese characters.

she puts away carefully in her school satchel. The teacher enters the classroom.

That evening, lying on her futon, M. cannot sleep. She stares fixedly at the neon lamp that has been switched off in the middle of the ceiling. In fact she feels very calm. She tries to remember everything she must do to prepare for her departure. The great departure. A little less than a week now. Then an end to all her frustrations. No more frustrated feelings about being different, more beautiful, more feeble, less intelligent or more intelligent. No more pressure, no more tension, no more anything. She tries to imagine once more what things will be like afterwards, but all she can visualize is nothingness, no more body, no more mind, no more society, no more people telling her she is 'sexy', no more malicious girls to bully her, no more tests, no more examinations, no more fear, no more anxiety about the future, no more anything. M. gives a little smile and falls asleep.

Wednesday, 1st July . . .

A young high-school girl killed herself yesterday evening by jumping off a ten-storey building. The victim was a minor, so we cannot publish her name.

This suicide marks the twenty-eighth of its kind this month. In a letter that was found in her school satchel laid beside her shoes on the edge of the terrace. . . .

Samurai

Rioshi Takahashi was thirty-six. He was rich – rich because his father, now dead, had been rich. He was still not married, preferring to take his time before saddling himself for life with some creature with whom he would have to share everything. His bank account would always allow him to marry some pretty little thing ten or fifteen years younger than himself and whom he could mould to his own satisfaction.

Friends of the family regularly tried to introduce him to promising young women. Sometimes he agreed to meet them, but this was mainly to indulge the sadistic pleasure he experienced in looking the girl over, and in watching her straining to present herself in the best light, affecting goody-goody airs of a well-brought-up young lady, putting on those timid, frightened expressions she knew men appreciated.

One of these days, he had promised his mother, he would make a decision, but for the moment all his attention was focused on the comfort of his own little personage.

In fact he was not so little, indeed he was even rather big for a Japanese, as his friends took pleasure in reminding him. He took advantage of his frequent visits to Europe to buy tailor-made clothes or to purchase accessories in London and Paris. Europeans themselves were no longer up to much, but their famous trade names had still kept the prestige Rioshi required to adorn the inner pocket of his jacket.

It was the same for the enormous and dazzling BMW he had just received in exchange for his old BM, which indeed was just as dazzling but perhaps a shade smaller, and which anyhow was not the very latest model. No, he just could not bring himself to tool around in a Mazda or a Toyota, all excellent vehicles no doubt, but in his view lacking in prestige.

He patronized the most famous hairdresser in Tokyo, who every ten days touched up the hair-style he had created for him. A style that was brushed straight back, the hair rather long and slightly brilliantined, cropped short round the ears. Whenever Rioshi looked at himself in a mirror, he always hoped to find he had an 'old British clubman' look, a sophisticated and decadent appearance he admired above all others.

Once a week, usually on Friday afternoons, he would spend a few hours in a men's beauty salon-cum-sauna, where he had himself massaged, pampered, manicured, burnished and bronzed. He enjoyed letting himself relax beneath the slim-fingered, expert, gentle hands which made him feel the whole world loved him. When he left the place, he felt ripe to take advantage of whatever opportunity might present itself.

Such was Rioshi's state of well-being that evening, as he stood in front of the sauna's glass and chrome façade, waiting for his BM to be brought up from the underground parking lot. His anthracite grey three-piece suit had just come from the cleaner's and the crimson of his necktie glowed softly like a last ember in a dying hearth. The attention he attracted and the speed with which he was attended to bolstered his consciousness of the effect his appearance produced. The air was cool and dry, as always in autumn after the extreme humidity of summer. Each year Rioshi made arrangements to spend the summer in Europe. He could not bear the clammy heat of Tokyo summers, the change from the air-conditioning of his office to the sticky sultriness of the street. So towards the beginning of every July he would depart for a tour of Europe, scouting new girls for his agency. For Rioshi's official position was president of a 'model' agency. The rents from the apartments and estates which his father had acquired during his lifetime were more than adequate to support the life-style Rioshi had adopted, but the idea of the agency, an idea put forward by his friend Norio, who liked to be called Ted, had appealed at once to Rioshi. It would allow him, under the guise of work, to be always surrounded by dream girls who, moreover, would all be dependent on his whims. He liked to think of these girls as belonging to his personal harem. A harem of girls who usually had blue eyes, blonde hair so soft to the touch, and such long legs. . . . With every fresh consignment he could take his pick and it was very rare for him not to get his way with one or two of them. They were not all idiots, but in fact he preferred them stupid – beautiful and stupid. He always took infinite delight in observing the envious faces of his cronies when he was parading one of his new conquests through the night streets of Tokyo. It was not easy to date one of those foreign women, even for rich young men like Rioshi's friends. Many of the girls would have nothing to do with Japanese men and preferred to sleep with other foreigners. Rioshi felt such utter contempt for them then. A racist, a full-blown racist. He knew he could never allow himself to marry one of them. They were all right for playing around with, yes, and for the enjoyment of those ever-provocative bodies, yes; but when it was a question of something serious like marriage, the lucky girl would be Japanese. Those foreign women were too free with their charms, too uncontrollable.

Rioshi slides into the camel-hair driving seat of his BM and allows the little chap in light grey livery to close the heavy door. Perfect matt sound of the door closing, like a bank safe. It gives Rioshi a thrill of pleasure, starting from the tips of his toes and running right up his spine. He shows a lordly indifference towards the little uniformed chap who, now bent double, is shouting polite nothings at the top of his voice, wishing him all the good in the world and begging him to favour the establishment with a return visit. Another little chap, also in light grey uniform, has joined the first in repeated bowings and scrapings. Rioshi, driving the BM out of the parking space, casts a glance in his rear mirror and sees the two silhouettes still bent double, arms at sides, caps in their right hands. That's what he appreciates here, the service, the respect for superiors. In Europe one would have to put oneself out, dispensing huge tips, and to have a well-known name in order to receive such special treatment. Especially in France, the personnel could be odious. It was no use Rioshi's renting the biggest limousines, staying at the best hotels, distributing copious largesse, he often caught a scornful look on the faces of the underlings. There were even some who pretended they did not understand English! Simply intolerable! No matter how much he paid for call-girls, he had the distinct impression that they were laughing at him. He had given fortunes to some of those girls, and they had not even been able to treat him as 'number one', *ichiban*, sovereign master. Here in Japan, whenever he visited a *toruko*, he always felt such a sense of his own importance; the girls played to perfection their role of professional slaves, they took their job seriously. Perhaps they were not so pretty, but they knew how to give value for money.

Rioshi considers for a few seconds the possibility of a visit to his favourite 'soapland', but dismisses the idea. This evening Ted-Norio has organized a little dinner with Tanaka-san, who owns three of the most celebrated discothèques in Tokyo and several restaurants that are doing well. There would also be three new girls, freshly arrived from Paris, and Ted-Norio has assured him that at least one of them would be to his liking.

She gives an idiotic smile and suddenly realizes it, opens her handbag to dig out a packet of Mild Seven. Her two companions are apparently busy exchanging endless jokes, for they never stop giggling like two high-school kids. Their strained but infectious laughter had brought to her lips that smile which made her look a complete imbecile. It is obvious she does not understand a single word of what those two gay dogs are saying. She lights up with studied gestures, using her brand-new Dupont lighter, and seizes the opportunity to take a look at herself in the mirror opposite. The greater part of its surface is covered with a retro advertisement extolling the benefits of that refreshing drink Coca-Cola. She glimpses one of her eyes in the circle of the o of Coca, part of the other in the a. Her nose is hidden under the thick red flourish underlining the word. Her lips, just underneath, are aglow with almost the same red.

The two men are taking another peek at the photos of her 'look', and from time to time the potential client raises his eyes from the glossy pages to rest them on Elizabeth's face, as if to check that everything is in place. Elizabeth likes her modelling career, but sometimes little things like that make her fume inside. She cannot stand being treated as a slab of butcher's meat over which customers hesitate among all the others wrapped in the same transparent plastic and lying on the same whitish polystyrene platter. 'That one looks a bit fatter but it's been better cut. . . .'

She has been particularly conscious of this kind of frustration ever since her arrival in Tokyo. Perhaps it is because of difficulties in communication and in understanding what is going on around her. As she grinds out her cigarette in the ashtray on the low table, she tries to think of other things. At that moment the other man addresses her in English: 'Mr Hana says you are wonderful. . . .' Elizabeth, turning towards the client, lets rip on him one of her devastating smiles. Mr Hana smiles back and she notices that all his front teeth are framed in gold, lending him a semi-golden, semi-ivory smile of a most fetching charm. . . .

'But in Japan, we Japanese prefer cute girls with . . . *nan dake*[13] . . . an innocent look.' He pronounces 'innocent' in a grandiloquent way, as if he has said 'renaissance'. 'Cute, you understand? Mr Hana would like to make sure that you would have that "look" in his photo. It's a publicity campaign for instant noodles, Cup Noodle.'

Elizabeth wonders just exactly what he expects of her, whether she should at once put on a completely candid expression, or else just show him that she is capable of delivering a 'cute' look, as 'cute' as he would wish. She

[13] *Nan dake*: Let's see.

wonders if she has got the job or if they are trying to tell her she is not suitable. In Paris she would have sensed immediately. Here, impossible. The client is still grinning at her with his gold and ivory teeth. But the eyes behind the steel-framed spectacles are not smiling. Elizabeth suddenly feels ill at ease, stupid and helpless. She leans towards her agent: 'Tell him I can fake it if necessary. . . .' The client, smile still clamped on his mouth, nods his head and she has the impression that he has guessed what she has just said.

The two men exchange a few formally polite expressions and collect almost simultaneously the business cards or 'name cards' they had produced at the start of the interview, tucking them away carefully in a little holder already full of other cards. Then they get to their feet – well, not exactly, for now they are bent double bowing to each other. Elizabeth also stands up, Mr Hana takes her hand and says in a timid, laboured French: 'Au revoir, Mademoiselle, et merci.'

Elizabeth hurriedly assumes a surprised, admiring and flattering look at such eloquence on the part of *monsieur*. They move towards the elevator. On her high heels she is a good head taller than both of them. While waiting for the elevator, further empty courtesies and salutations are exchanged, a relaxing of tension after the strained concentration of the interview. The doors open, and until they close the little man keeps bowing and displaying all that gold-ivory cloisonné-work dentition.

Elizabeth opens the door to her minuscule apartment and at once pushes the ventilation button in the toilet that is just on her left.

'David, I've *told* you not to shut that thing. You want to get me run in or what?' She shuts the front door and leaves the toilet door open. The noise of the ventilator and the smallness of the bathroom give the impression of a ship's cabin.

David, stretched out on the bed that covers nearly all the surface area of the apartment, gazes at the ceiling and does not stir an inch. Elizabeth dumps her big bag in a corner, works her way round the foot of the bed to the cooknook and puts water on to boil.

'You might at least ask me how it went.'

'How did it go?'

'Actually, I don't know. You never know. What about you, what did you do today?'

'Nothing.'

For some time now David has adopted a completely negative attitude. It is one year since he arrived in Tokyo. He's always saying he's going to leave, but he keeps putting it off. He has twice left Japan to spend two or three days in Hong Kong in order to renew his visa. When Elizabeth set eyes on him for the first time she was at once attracted by him. He was handsome, with a handsomeness different from the other male models who were generally too immature, too perfect, or too something or other. But he preserves a constant sort of detachment towards whatever is going on around him.

She goes and lies down beside him and gently takes from his lips the tiny joint, which she stubs out in the ashtray beside the bed. David does not move, his eyes still fixed on the ceiling. Elizabeth, her head resting on the arm bent behind his head, looks at him for some time before saying: 'What's the matter, David? Speak to me.'

She is determined to make him snap out of his mute indifference, which is driving her crazy. He is Swedish but has a fluent command of English, French and German. After only one year in Japan, he can conduct a conversation in Japanese. He is twenty-eight and working as a model in order one day to be able to fulfil his dream of making his own film. He has studied at the Beaux-Arts in Paris, and that is where they met. Then he decided to travel and they got together again in Tokyo. She had succeeded in obtaining a contract with one of the best agencies in the capital.

'What do you say we leave and get right away from here, far away from it all. . . . Kristel was telling me about this beach in Thailand. . . .'

David gets up and takes a couple of steps into the doll's house bathroom, where he locks himself in.

Rioshi parks his BM outside the entrance to the night-club. The uniformed boy is there just for that, to keep places vacant for high-class visitors, and also to greet the famous or the rich – or both. The young boy bows to Rioshi and Rioshi adores that. He also adores hearing his name followed by the suitably formal greetings. A few *gaijin*[14] entering at the same time turn to look at him. Out of the corner of his eye he sees one of the girls, tall and blonde, bending to whisper to her woman friend, just as tall but a little less blonde: 'Who is he?'

Rioshi descends the stairs, and the further he descends, the more the decibel level rises. The manager of the club recognizes him at once, bows to him and tells him that his boss is waiting. He takes the heavy overcoat that Rioshi had casually draped round his shoulders, entrusts it to the baby doll behind her counter, and asks Rioshi to follow him. But on the way he stops beside a group of three

---

[14] *Gaijin*: foreigner.

foreigners who are having a lively argument with another manager. The latter, in pop-star costume ablaze with sequins, his hair brilliantined and his eyes indignant, is drawing himself up to his not very considerable height. His face reveals the full seriousness of the situation. The *gaijin* seem to be furious.

'What's going on?' Rioshi asks the first manager, who is still standing beside him.

'They say they're models, and that they left their portfolios here last time, but Hiroshi doesn't remember them, and so he doesn't want to let them enter without paying.'

The system in the fashionable night-spots in Tokyo is to allow any model who works for an agency to enter free of charge and order free drinks. That attracts business, and creates an atmosphere, especially when the models are girls with long legs who act crazy. It is good for business. Rioshi smiles and indicates to the manager that he is ready to follow him: 'A *gaijin* will always try to gatecrash.'

The manager makes his way rapidly through the throng, sometimes pushing people out of the way. Rioshi follows him. All these little nobodies who work in this kind of club adopt the same contemptuous attitude towards foreigners, though that does not stop them from trying every trick in the trade to get one of these tall girls into bed with them. To be able to talk about it next day with one's cronies, with precise details, confers prestige. Rioshi understands their feelings exactly – they have a right to all they can get.

The manager has opened a door to a sound-proof private room. There are a few reserved tables, and a gigantic video screen. An old James Dean movie is running without the sound-track, but the muted thumping of the amplifiers next door can still be felt through the wall.

One side of the room is one enormous window, also sound-proofed, which allows a view of the action on the dance floor, so that one can see and be seen.

The friends stand up and their eager greetings burst forth, a little too loud, too knowing, too Americanized. Three girls remain seated, but their faces are turned towards Rioshi. All three are smiling. On the table there is a bottle of champagne whose neck leaning out of the ice-bucket says *Moet et Chandon*. Rioshi sits down in the place they have made for him on the red velvet banquette. Introductions are made. There are two French girls and one English. One of the French girls is exactly Rioshi's type. She looks *so* 'European'. That is, according to the ideas the Japanese harbour about what constitutes 'European'. She appears sophisticated and de luxe, perfectly at ease, holding her champagne glass as if that had been her sole occupation all her life. Her long legs are crossed and encased in a tight skirt that leaves part of one thigh exposed. Black tights. She seems to be bored, and that only adds to her charm. The discussion is going on in English. In fact there is no real discussion, only exchanges of words.

Ted-Norio bends towards Rioshi and whispers in Japanese: 'What did I tell you? Get a load of those tits.' Actually, Rioshi has not looked at the girl's breasts, which is unusual, for that is what he always does first.

When David enters the club he wants to smash everything. He who was so quiet a type . . . a pacifist. . . . Those debates in Paris. . . . 'Peace' for the whole world. No more atom bombs. The demos . . . and now he feels he could smash someone's face in. Why? How could this have happened? The country, these people, they get on your nerves. You cannot say why, but that's how it is. He has tried to explain his feelings to his friend Kris, who has just arrived from Sweden, but Kris couldn't understand why he was up in arms against such nice people. 'They are so kind and polite. The girls laugh all the time. And they're so sweet. . . .' Kris has just stepped off the plane. It's useless to try explaining to someone who has just stepped off the plane. More than in any other land, society here oppresses him, makes him feel he is suffocating. And as if in some bad dream he is sinking deeper, he cannot extricate himself from this glutinous mass that is closing over his head. He looks straight in the eye of the absurd little manager who steps aside to let him pass but does not greet him. David is well known, famous even. Because of his blond hair, his blue eyes, his wild look, he has made three commercials for television. Here the television is Mount Olympus, and if one plays around on it, one cannot but be a god. Sometimes if you get a good look at the faces of the gods in question . . . mere puppets manipulated to make the kids laugh or to frighten them. But they are seen on television, so. . . .

David makes straight for the bar without responding to the enthusiastic cries of 'Hello', 'Bon soir' and 'Konbanwa'[15] that break out all round him. These little geese of seventeen who think they're stars as soon as they get their spoilt brat's pout on the cover of some cheap and rubbishy magazine. He orders a double tequila. The barman, got up like the room boy of a grand hotel, rushes to pour his tequila with precise and hurried gestures before asking David's neighbour what he wants. David takes his glass and returns to the centre of the room.

It is one o'clock in the morning. The dance floor is packed. Filled to bursting with the most diverse mugs and modes. A mixed, cosmopolitan lot. It is mainly the *gaijin*

---

[15] 'Konbanwa': 'Good evening'.

who stand out, making the most of their inches in order to appear still taller. They exchange smiles as they dance. Among them the more moderately sized, more drab Japanese. They are in their own land, yet they look as if they do not want to intrude. In fact they are not really at home here. They have simply been granted permission to participate in Tokyo's Great Foreigner Festival. And the Foreigner enters into the game good-naturedly, the Foreigner pure and simple. What a bunch of clots! David is about to return to the bar when he glimpses Elizabeth through the glass partition at the end of the room. When she had stormed out banging the door she had shouted that she was going to live her life to the full, because she had only one. Elizabeth is the one person to whom he would be able to explain his feelings. Yet this evening he has succeeded only in putting her back up. And now there she is behaving like a silly little goose with her champagne glass in her hand. Her dazzling magazine-cover smile painted bright red across her face. But he knows she is not as brainless as the rest. In any case that kind of shit rubs off on you whoever you are. He sees she's a little drunk. All round her (she is standing, as if making a speech or a toast), all round her, lower down, faces lifted towards her, half a dozen or so people. He recognizes two friends of Elizabeth, girls working for the same agency. The rest are men in dark suits cut in the latest fashion . . . same hairstyles, club regulars, local playboys.

David turns his face away in disgust. He tries to get interested in the pretty blonde giving him the glad eye or the little Japanese doll dancing right next to him, seemingly totally absorbed by the jerky music which rhythms her painstakingly correct steps. Yet he senses that she is giving herself up to him body and soul. He returns to the agitated bartender and orders another double tequila.

The click of the closing door rouses Rioshi from sleep. With his left hand he feels the rumpled sheets beside him. He opens one eye and rolls his still-sleeping body to the side. Thus his face comes in contact with the hollow in the pillow where Elizabeth's scent still lingers. The spicy fragrance unleashes a sequence of images in Rioshi's mind. He closes his eyes again – what a woman! Scored once again! No, better than that! Rioshi slides his hand towards the pillow as if he wanted to caress the hair that had been spread all over it.

Suddenly on the girl's face is superimposed that of the boy. . . . Such an expressive face. He had come over to speak to Elizabeth, had said a few words, then just looked at her. The change had been so striking that Rioshi had thought he should intervene. But when the boy had looked at him in turn, he had felt so small, so ridiculous, so insignificant, that he felt a sudden surge of fury. The club's chuckers-out had hurried up to them in case they had to break it up, but the big blond boy had simply turned his majestic back upon him, leaving behind a girl on the verge of tears and a powerless, infuriated Rioshi.

In an angry outburst Elizabeth had snapped that if he 'smoked' less, he would be more sociable. In order to convince himself that he still retained some vestige of power, he had quietly called the manager and asked him to do something about the matter. Rioshi had felt his self-confidence restored, he had regained face. He had felt like a *yakuza*[16] issuing orders to one of his right-hand men. The fate of a man hung on a few words. The manager had adopted a knowing air, playing along with him.

Rioshi the samurai. Rioshi has always admired the no-

---

[16] *Yakuza*: gangster.

bility of the samurai. The quiet strength. His power. . . . Yet his own family, as far back as it could be traced, had never been more than Osaka merchants. Merchants, the opposite of the samurai. This morning, when he had finally succeeded in getting Elizabeth into his BM, he had felt he was rediscovering that sense of conquest, of victory, he usually experienced at such times. But with this girl, it was different.

She was beautiful, she was drunk. . . . When he had possessed her, it was as if she had given nothing of herself. He had not felt that impression of samurai domination, of superiority, that he usually felt. That bitter after-taste, that spasm of disgust when, their rompings ended, he would find himself confronted with a creature he had succeeded in wrecking, whom he had fully intended to destroy. Nothing of all that this morning. Instead, as he awoke, that man's face superimposing itself on the girl's.

Rioshi looks at the little digital clock standing on his bedside table: 2.13 p.m.

The situation has been evolving. . . .

David is more and more cut off from society, seems more and more unhappy. Elizabeth loves him more and more, realizes she cannot live without him, that her whole life revolves round him. She is pregnant.

Rioshi sees Elizabeth as often as possible, cannot do without her, has no eyes now for other girls. David's face still haunts his dreams and his imagination. He discovers with horror that he has never felt for a woman what he feels now for this man. He tries not to think about him. He is very attentive, he wants to help Elizabeth who will help David. He wants to become their friend. Never before has he felt any desire to be friends with anyone. The life he has lived until now disgusts him. He feels sick, guilty and wretched.

'Rioshi, I would never have thought you could become my friend. I don't know what I would have done if you hadn't been there.'

'It was good for me, too. Enormously. I don't know why or how, but there it is – in a few weeks I've become a different man, thanks to you. How is David?'

'Still the same . . . our child, I wonder what it represents for him. When I gave him the news, his eyes started shining, shining. A brilliance such as I had never seen in his eyes before. And then it died out. It was like the last sputtering of a candle.'

'I know what you mean, I remember you told me so.'

Elizabeth stubbed out her Mild Seven in the tiny white ashtray on the little black table of the café where they liked to meet.

'I'll finish this packet and stop smoking.'

Rioshi enters the club and looks around. He is looking for Tanaka-san, who has made an appointment to meet him here. The décor has not changed, yet it is no longer the same place: it will never be the same place again. Automatically he takes the double Scotch with water brought to him on a little tray. The young waiter waits for some gesture of thanks for having remembered his favourite drink. Rioshi gives him a faint smile. But his smile becomes fixed when he sees the manager approaching, all smiles too, an obviously satisfied look on his face. Rioshi's fear turns to panic when he hears what the other has to say, when he hears what he had been so afraid of hearing. The little soldier has carried out his orders. The words, the attitude he had taken that evening – it all floods back into his memory. He had forgotten. He had never believed that this man would have taken him at his word. He could never have believed that this underling would have been capable of carrying out such tactics in order to satisfy an important client, a friend of the boss. A promotion, perhaps, the pleasure of a duty performed. The pleasure of carrying out orders. Idiocy and stupidity. He is still smiling away, surprised not to see more satisfaction in the other's face. Rioshi tries to stay calm and does some quick thinking.

'When's it for?' he manages to say, his voice hoarse.

'For this evening perhaps.'

Rioshi puts his drink down untasted and goes towards the hat-check counter. His legs feel weak as water and the way in which the little hat-check girl stares at him tells him his face is drawn and distorted. He dashes out of the club, jumps into his BM, zooms off, cutting right in front of a taxi, which blows an indignant horn. There is still a slight chance. Rioshi drives as fast as the traffic, dense at that hour, will allow. He takes a lot of risks but not too many all the same so as not to be booked by the cops at every crossing. The cops, David. . . . He couldn't bear it. Rioshi again sees David's face before him, his throat tightens. He accelerates. When he turns the corner of the little street, the flashing red lights on two white ambulances with black stripes herald the full extent of the catastrophe.

He climbs the steps of the narrow staircase three at a time, arrives outside the door of Elizabeth's apartment. It is wide open, partly blocked by a broad, navy-blue back with a diagonal leather belt. A youthful face that is nevertheless totally lacking in youth turns towards him. 'Who are you?' Rioshi answers in a tone of voice as impolite as that used by the cop, letting him know his place. The cop has had time to weigh up Rioshi. His expensive clothes, his self-assurance. The Tokyo police chief is a friend of Rioshi's mother. The young cop at once changes his tone and his attitude. He explains that Rioshi cannot enter the apartment and again asks him, but much more politely, to reveal his identity.

'I'm a friend of the people who live here. I'm also a friend of Mr Namakawa.' Another cop has come out to join the young one at the door. He is older and has heard Rioshi's reply.

'Do you speak English?' he asks.

'Yes.'

'Could you help us?'

'All I want is to help my friends.'

The room is bathed in a strange light, because the bedside lamp has been overturned and is now lying on its side on the floor, casting weird shadows on the walls and the ceiling. An atmosphere of some old English film. The ending had to be sad! Rioshi suddenly sees Elizabeth crouching in a corner. Her pleading face turns towards him, her eyes have a curious glitter and she is breathing noisily. He is about to rush towards her when he notices David, or at least David's back, because after what must have been a brief scuffle David is stuck between the bed and the wall. Another young cop, who has lost his cap, has his knee between David's shoulder-blades. A perfect aikido or judo immobilization technique. The young cop looks pleased with himself. His spectacles are slightly askew but his eyes are sparkling, his mouth still a bit tense, his nostrils dilated.

'What do you think you're doing?'

The young cop does not relax his hold and goes on staring at the nape of David's neck. David's face looks crumpled, his mouth twisted, open in a slavering rictus.

The oldest of the cops answers Rioshi's question: 'He tried to escape. . . .' He hesitates a moment, then continues, rather as if he were making an official report to his superior: 'He was found in the act of smoking illegal substances.' He uses the official term used in newspapers to indicate marijuana.

Now Rioshi notices a third intruder busy turning out the drawers of the small white chest of drawers.

'But you're hurting him!' And he reaches out to grab the judoka-cop's shoulder.

His arm feels very painful and the cop's knee in the small of his back makes it difficult to breathe. The hairs of the carpet are tickling his nostrils and make him want to sneeze. He can vaguely hear voices behind him. He understands a few words from time to time but cannot make out everything that's said. He recognizes the voice of Elizabeth's boy-friend. The one who always looks at him with frightened eyes. Crypto-homo. A poor type. I shouldn't like to be in his shoes.

But apparently he seems to be making a favourable impression on the cops. From the tone of his voice. The general atmosphere. Suddenly the judo hold is released, the weight is off his back. The first thing he does is to rub the end of his nose vigorously. It is a very pleasant sensation. Then he begins gently to massage his painful shoulder, but already they are pulling on his arms and there is a metallic click as the steel handcuffs are snapped on his wrists in front of him. He is still on his knees and these two pieces of metal are shining brightly. In their convex mirror he sees his face all shrunken and deformed. In that reflection he also sees that he will never be able to endure what is about to happen to him.

Society – that stupid lout – revels in this kind of affair whenever it gets a chance. He has done wrong, so he must pay. He will be swept away on the endless rapids of the bureaucratic process. Bureaucracy. His own powerlessness.

Forced to submit. Forced to play into their hands if he wants to survive. . . . He will end up in prison. Prison. And he has always felt like a prisoner. Prisoner of one thing or another. . . . And he will have to endure all that in order to survive. Survive. . . .

Now he is being forced to stand up. All at once Elizabeth is holding him. Her tearful face is pressed against his. Her burning lips seek his mouth, slide down to his neck. She is murmuring things he cannot follow. They try to separate the pair. Elizabeth reacts strongly. She begins screaming. The cops are at a loss: they do not dare touch her. They have an awkward, embarrassed, clumsy look. He sees the path is clear. David rushes forward. Elizabeth stops screaming, and behind him he hears the grunts of the cops who have also started to run. A wild pack. Hounds bounding after some little frightened creature. He is outside. The cold air a slap in the face. He is about to race down the narrow stairs when he hears the tramp of heavy boots rushing up from below. At once he turns and dashes up some iron stairs, four at a time. The staircase, shaking under the weight of David and the mob now chasing close behind him, begins to vibrate, re-echoing in the darkness with a strange musical sound. Despite his handcuffed arms that keep him off balance he keeps his lead and soon comes out under a starry sky. A huge white moon is gleaming like an enormous cultured pearl in its jewel-case of black velvet. The metallic noise of the footsteps drawing nearer pounds in his head. Small, evanescent clouds of breath come from his panting mouth. Reminding him of the bulls he used to go and see in his grandfather's meadows at dawn, their big muzzles and the fuming jets of warm breath issuing from them.

He rushes towards the edge of the terrace but is stopped short, his throat suddenly choking, racked by the effort to catch his breath. The violence of the pain makes him howl like a savage beast. His cry has a weird sound in the night. He has run into a wire washing-line, but he manages to stumble free of it and run towards the low parapet. Over his shoulder he glimpses, level with the last step, a cap with a huge metal badge on the front. He jumps on the parapet. The street down below looks so very tiny. He feels as if he is looking down on a doll's house world. The roof of the neighbouring building is too far away for him to jump across to it. He turns round now and sees them, all the others, advancing on him in the arc of a circle. They are moving slowly now. Behind them, Rioshi appears, shouting: 'Don't go near him or he'll jump!' David gets the message and realizes that he had never intended to jump. Yet the cops have stopped and are watching him fixedly. Stopped dead. David notices that except for the oldest one they are all wearing glasses. He finds this detail amusing. The one who had got him down on the carpet has drawn his truncheon and holds it in front of him like a kendo stick, like a sword. In the pose of a samurai. David's eyes try to find in his face some vestige of humanity, something interesting or touching, something that will restore his love for the human race, something that will explain why. . . . Something, no matter what. The cop, finding himself thus observed, has an obviously automatic reflex, gives a little hissing cry of 'Oosh', slides his right foot forward and raises his truncheon a little higher. David, caught off balance by this movement, steps back towards the right and loses his footing. He makes a last attempt to regain his balance by trying to spread his arms, but these are inexorably tied by those stupid, ugly rings. . . .

David was standing there. Now there is nothing but a black emptiness, a black emptiness strewn with stars but black and empty all the same. The little cop has not altered his stance, his head has simply tilted a little to the left. He has the astonished look of a puppy who has just burst a carnival balloon with a pat from his fat little paw. 'It was there and now there's nothing!' The three others lean over the parapet. Their chests leaning on its edge, their feet do not reach the ground.

Rioshi cannot look away from this ridiculous spectacle, though his eyes are filled with tears. Eventually he looks at the man with the truncheon. He stares him full in the face. He wants to stamp that face completely on his memory. He wants to be sure never to forget it . . . never to forget what it represents and never again to be a part of what it represents. He hears Elizabeth's light footsteps coming towards him. He turns and rushes forward to stop her before she can reach the open terrace.

The baby has now been born. His papa Rioshi is the happiest of men. His mother Elizabeth smiled when they showed her the baby all wrinkled and grimacing. Her first smile for months and months.

Rioshi's mother is glad to have a grandson, but her son's marriage with a foreigner has upset her considerably. And with a tall blonde who never smiles, never speaks, who does nothing, who just keeps staring in front of her. Her son looks after her so well! He had insisted upon marrying her as soon as possible. And to think she had once introduced him to some of the best marriage prospects in Tokyo. . . . How he has changed!

Rioshi is happy. He has decided to call the baby Ichiro, which means 'first son'. He had hoped so much for a baby with blue eyes and blond hair.

All for My Child or Noriko

Teenage girls in high-school gym costumes, their navy-blue pleated dresses lifted up. Spreadeagled in provocative poses. Ropes, candles, bondaged flesh, bodies whipped, contorted, ravished. Her fingers turn the pages of cheap paper and each one reveals even more vulgar drawings, more violent. The girls' faces have frightened expressions, submissive, resigned to their fate. The boys' faces have a demented glow. Lips twisted in a sadistic rictus. In the balloons, onomatopoeic exclamations, insults, barked commands batter the reader, tease him. The Chinese characters in brilliant black jump off the page, starkly outlined on the greyish white of the coarse paper.

Noriko closes the little magazine whose extravagantly coloured cover contrasts with the matt pages inside. She puts it back carefully in the drawer at the bottom of the desk. She makes sure she has covered it with the big geographical *Atlas of the World*, the Japanese-English dictionary and the diary bound in black leather, in the same order as she had found them. Then she stands up slowly, pushes the little chair back under the desk, gives everything a final look. . . . Everything is in order in the tiny room. She goes out, closing the door softly behind her.

Noriko sits down in front of her cup of tea. The little living-room is sunny and bright. Outside, an itinerant tofu vendor is blowing his plangent trumpet. She needs to think. The images she has just seen up there in her son's room have not shocked her . . . not all that much. . . . What has shocked her is the realization that her suspicions were well founded. When she decided to search the drawers of Hitoshi's desk, she already knew what she would discover. She did not know what form it would take, but she sensed she would find the irrefutable proof of her child's sexual frustration. For some time now she had been observing him even more carefully than usual. . . . Watching him gazing fixedly at television, distractedly swallowing his favourite dishes, abandoning his computer games. From these signs she had concluded that her son was in danger. That her son's whole future lay in the balance. After so many years of training, shaping, educating. As a child, what a dear little fellow! How proud she had been of him right from the start. Photos of Hitoshi in a kimono for the Children's Festival, the *sangoshichi* or three-five-seven,[17] the ages celebrated on that day. So perfect. Adorable. Everything was so easy then. All that mattered was that he should be clean, obedient, polite, cute.

Noriko recalled the passion with which she had thrown herself into the education of her only son. She wanted him to become someone people looked up to, someone with a real life of his own, with decisions to be made, responsibilities. Someone with access to all that was best, all that

---

[17] Usually known as *shichigosan* (seven-five-three), the festival is on 15 November.

was greatest in Japanese society. She knew what had to be done in order to reach such heights. Her son would enter Japan's most prestigious university – Tokyo University. She could remember clearly when, one night, lying beside her snoring husband stinking of sake, she had made herself this promise, defining the whole aim of her life. From now on, nothing else counted. Everything would revolve round that fixed idea. She set to work like an architect preparing the foundations of a new building. She drew up plans and sought the means to realize them.

School first of all. The school in which he would begin his studies would determine his future course in life. Her son was intelligent, at any rate just as intelligent as most boys of his age. It was necessary to give him a good start, give him access to privileges, place his foot in the stirrup.

She found the money for it. She economized on the family budget. She cut down on her husband's pocket-money and made him agree that they did not really need to trade in their car every two years, that it was all for their son's future. Anyhow, there was no need to explain things, except as a formality. The education of their child was her business, and hers alone.

The next problem was to keep an enthusiasm for study alive in Hitoshi. When he arrived home exhausted, washed out after the evening classes, and he still had to put in two or three hours of application and concentration, what an effort she had had to make herself in order to try to help him, to encourage him, to keep alive the dream of Todai,[18] the prestigious university. . . . What a battle she had had to wage with herself not to give in and just let him watch his favourite programme on television, or simply let him sleep.

---

[18] Todai: a common contraction of 'Tokyo Daigaku', or Tokyo University.

She became as well informed as he in most of his subjects. She simply followed the courses through the medium of her son. Team-work relations were established between mother and son. Noriko was excellent at giving every task a competitive edge that stimulated the boy and made him attack his studies as another boy of his age would throw himself into a game. But the problem which very soon became of prime importance was that of leisure time. Noriko, despite her efficiency in fixing a timetable, could not allow Hitoshi enough free time to enable him to play in a normal fashion. The less opportunity he had of playing with friends of his own age, the more he retreated into himself, practising computer games on his little machine, a present for his efforts in maths. Noriko had noticed a certain falling-off in that most important of all subjects and had proposed this computer prize contest in order to motivate her pupil. This stratagem had borne fruit, since Hitoshi now obtained excellent marks in maths, better in fact than in all other subjects.

So Noriko had been able to face up to all the obstacles life had tried to put between her son and Todai University. The latest one to rear its ugly head was sex. Although Noriko was psychologically prepared for this difficulty, she felt as if she had been taken utterly by surprise when she noticed that her son had become a little man and was beginning to respond to the attractions of women.

It was a Sunday evening, and, as on all Sunday evenings at that hour, Hitoshi was allowed to watch a variety programme aimed specially at Japanese adolescents. They could see their favourite boy and girl 'idol' singers on it. Hitoshi and Noriko had just finished dinner. Father had still not returned from his game of golf. He must have stayed on at the club to eat and drink with his colleagues from the office, who were also his Sunday golf partners.

As was his custom, Hitoshi had propped himself against

the wall with three or four floor cushions, and, slumped there like a pasha, was watching the small portable television placed on the low table. Noriko, seated beside another low table, was letting her cup of hot green tea cool a little and also watching the television programme. She took advantage of it to watch her boy out of the corner of her eye. It was a real examination. She had developed this habit of scrutinizing the little creature upon whom she had pinned all her hopes and ambitions. The little creature had indeed grown up. He was a good head and shoulders taller than Noriko and had shot up recently. He had firm cheeks and the brush cut of his hair exposed a powerful neck and fleshy ears. Long eyelashes still lent his face a juvenile and somewhat feminine look. He was just fifteen. His head was held slightly back, leaning against the wall, and his half-closed eyes let the images of the little screen filter into his consciousness. It gave him a very relaxed and blasé attitude. When the show was over, he would go back to work for at least two hours. On Sundays, she tried to hold him to a more flexible timetable.

While she was lost in contemplation of her son's face, his features underwent a spectacular change, his eyes opened wide and took on a terrifying fixity, his nose became slightly pinched but at the same time the nostrils dilated. The ears turned a hot red and seemed even more fleshy. Noriko was on the point of asking him if he felt all right, when she understood what was happening. On the small screen, a young, fresh face. A pouting mouth, mischievous and innocent all at the same time. Eyes laughing, sparkling. Chunky lips. The young girl singer was swaying to the rhythm of her number, making her short, fluffy dress swing and float around her wasp waist. Slim legs shod in little black ballerina slippers were gracefully undulating. Noriko felt sick. She was now openly gazing at the young animal her son had become. Hitoshi had noticed his mother looking at him. Their two glances had met briefly and then, although he seemed to have again become absorbed in his television programme, his eyes no longer registered what they were looking at. His mind was directed entirely towards his mother, who had caught him out, who had understood. His scarlet ears seemed to be beating slightly beneath the pressure of blood that had rushed to his head.

That night, lying beside her husband who had returned home completely knocked out by his day in the open air followed by an evening spent drinking with his colleagues, Noriko was wondering what to do. A score of times, a hundred times, she turned things over in her mind. It always came down to the same problem, clear and inexorable. If Hitoshi relaxed his concentration even just a fraction, his entry to Todai would be severely threatened. Even if he kept hard at work all the time, the battle would be a tough one, very tough. If Hitoshi's mind were distracted from the effort by something as obsessive as sexual attraction, his chances of succeeding would be dramatically diminished. Thinking of all those years spent with books, all those hours of study, of research, of anxiety, Noriko could not hold back two tears that slid slowly from the corner of her eyes and down her cheeks.

Next day she redoubled her vigilance, but was even more smiling and attentive than usual. Hitoshi, who perhaps was expecting some strong reaction, even a reprimand from his mother, at first looked ill at ease, but with the absence of any threatening signs he gradually relaxed and forgot the incident. Yet Noriko continued to keep an eye on him, and day by day it was revealed how justified were here fears. Her son was undoubtedly distracted from his studies by something very powerful that was attacking him from inside. He began to ask her for more free time to go shopping in the big commercial centres of Shibuya and Shinjuku. He would come back all excited, and she sensed that she was losing him. . . . In the evenings she noticed he came home a little later than usual.

One day, watching for his return from the window of her bedroom on the first floor, she understood why. She caught sight of Hitoshi in his black school uniform. His peaked cap had been pushed back on his head, and he had an arm through only one of the straps of his satchel. A little gangling in his walk, from a distance he also looked relaxed. He was strolling along quite nonchalantly. It was a contrived pose to give the impression of someone who knows what's what, and whom nothing can surprise any more. As she gazed in astonishment at this son she no longer recognized, Noriko noticed something very disturbing. A few steps in front of Hitoshi, perhaps a dozen yards away, a young high-school girl was walking. The girl must also have been about fifteen or sixteen, and the little dazzling white bobby socks set off the matt brown of her bare legs. The pleated navy-blue dress and the middy blouse with its sailor collar gave her a wholesome and serious appearance. Her figure was slim and graceful. She was walking slightly bent to one side, the side of her large, heavy satchel, which seemed to be dragging on her frail arm.

Noriko had recognized the young daughter of a neighbour who lived two or three houses away. She had met her mother a few times at the supermarket. The young girl was attending a school much further away than Hitoshi's, so she came home later than he did: that was why he had started returning later. He was waiting for the girl. For the pleasure of seeing her, of walking a few steps behind her. As if nothing were the matter, naturally. Noriko began to calculate all the energy her son must have dispensed in tracking down the girl. In studying her times of arrival and departure, waiting without seeming to be waiting for her, dying to speak to her, to laugh with her, to touch her. Once again, Noriko began to feel quite sick. As when one has drunk too much or eaten too copiously and one forces oneself to swallow a last mouthful, a last glass. . . . All that wasted time when he could have been applying himself to study, to the building of his future. All those lost moments dreaming of that sweet face, those almond eyes and that skin, so silky smooth. She imagined him tossing and turning in his bed. Trying in vain to fall asleep – that restorative sleep he needs so badly in order to face up to the coming day. Now Noriko's eyes were filled with tears . . . tears of rage. It wasn't right! When the goal was so close. . . . She felt so terribly helpless. But was she really? Was there not some way of avoiding disaster? Had she not in former days overcome obstacles which at first had appeared insurmountable? Gradually calm returned to her and, wiping away the traces of tears that had dried on her cheeks, she went to the front door to greet her son.

'Tadaima.'[19]

'O kaerinasai.'[20]

The ritual phrases re-echoed in the little corridor. Hitoshi, having slung his satchel on the first step of the stairs, as always, divests himself of his outdoor shoes, puts on the house slippers that have been put out ready for his return, opens the refrigerator to take a bottle of Coca-Cola. Every day it's the same scenario. He uncaps the bottle that releases a grateful 'pschiff'. Then, head thrown back, he takes long gulps of the drink and moves towards the table where his evening meal is awaiting him. His mother

---

[19] 'Here I am!' [20] 'Welcome back home!'

too. Yet there is only one rice-bowl. She will just wait until her husband telephones to say that he will not be home for dinner. Beside the bowl of rice, another, smaller, with a lid which Hitoshi takes off. A slight cloud of steam rises to the ceiling. He seizes this bowl and noisily slurps a mouthful of *miso* soup.[21] He burns his tongue. On a plate, a sort of fried hamburger. Hitoshi dowses it generously with ketchup and, taking it between his two chopsticks, lifts it to his mouth and bites into it. He replaces the thing with a big bite taken out of it on top of the white rice, some of whose grains become stained a blood red. He knows his mother is waiting until he has almost finished his meal to ask him about his day.

Waiting is what she is doing now. Seated demurely in front of her eternal cup of green tea. Her legs are folded to one side, all the weight of her body resting on one thigh and one arm propped on the tatami of the little living-room. Her white apron protects a blouse with big black polka dots and a skirt in grey and black herring-bone pattern. Her feet in the transparent beige of her tights appear tiny, her hair is cut short and lightly waved. She resembles exactly one of those housewifely mothers who are interviewed on television when they praise to high heaven the peculiar virtues of a certain washing powder or washing-up liquid. She is watching her big son eat and, truly, she is waiting; but this time she is not waiting impatiently to know if the maths test has gone off well or if Hitoshi has obtained good marks in the true-or-false history test. Of course these are the questions she has to ask him. But really her mind is occupied by other problems, by other questions she will never ask. Such as, how long has he been suffering from this sickness that is

---

[21] Soup made from fermented bean paste, a traditional dish.

consuming him? From this physical urge he does not know how to satisfy? She tries to recapitulate. The falling-off in his studies represents the most deplorable effect of this inner malaise. Each time she comes upon him day-dreaming in front of an open book. When he loiters on his way home. Hours wasted poring over magazines of the kind she has found in his room. The newspaper kiosks are awash with them, and in bookshops she often sees young boys standing and looking through their favourite porno mags. She has intensified her explorations and is always on the look-out for new issues in his desk. Sometimes he keeps one of them week after week, but in general she finds a new number every week. She assumes that he gets rid of them one by one in a trash-box on the way to school. He must have got everything well organized, to Noriko's great displeasure, by excluding her completely from all that part of his life. It is becoming unbearable. A kind of revulsion, or rather loathing, overwhelms her at the sight of her great slob of a son. But very quickly this feeling is replaced by a vague pity for this young animal in the grip of unconquerable forces.

She reflects upon her own experience of life. Girls and boys react differently to that kind of problem, but it is basically the same. She recalls that period in her life when she really felt the need to be with someone of the opposite sex. The first time was after she had entered the Toho young ladies' college; she was just eighteen.

Until then, all had been normal: going out with high-school girl-friends, eating American ice-creams after classes. There were parties attended only by young girls. They did talk a little about boys, but did not really dare to look at them. They discussed also those very rare girls who had a *coïbito*, a sort of boy-friend with whom they were 'going steady'. They were indeed rare birds, with unusual experiences. They were rather admired, and rather feared, because they were 'different'. They tried to imagine what they might be feeling, what sort of lives they led. It was both very exciting and very frustrating. Nobody dared believe it would happen to her one day.

Noriko lifts her teacup to her lips and takes a genteel little sip. Memories come back to her, like images that suddenly appear on a television screen when it is just switched on. She sees herself walking down the wide avenue on the campus bordered by the university buildings. She has just started her first year at university. After the agony of the entrance exams – 'examination hell', as it is called – she feels free as a bird. She is still living with her parents, but she can return home at whatever hour she pleases, as long as it is before eleven-thirty. Often when she is at a party that looks like finishing later than usual, she telephones her parents to let them know she will be sleeping at a girl-friend's house near the centre of Tokyo. That spares her the horrors of the last train transporting to the suburbs its nightly cargo of human wrecks, slumped snoring on the seats or suspended from their plastic rings like sides of beef, rocked to and fro by the movements of the train, playing Casanova, spluttering and spitting, and trying to pick up girls on their own. Shameless, some do not even bother to hide from the rest of the carriage (eyes trying not to see, to look elsewhere) how they try to fondle girls who do not know how to escape their attentions. So her parents are only too glad to accept the alternative of a night spent at the girl-friend's house.

That particular day she is walking down the university's main avenue when someone touches her lightly on the arm. She swings round, expecting to find a well-known face, but on the contrary the face means nothing to her. He has a lovely big smile, but she does not know him. The eyes are looking at her frankly and sparkling with fun. The features are regular, charming. 'Would you like to help the Cambodian refugees?' Under her nose he shakes a metal box with a slot for money and covered with messages encouraging people to support the refugees. In one corner there is a photograph of some wretched child. Without thinking she digs into her handbag, looking for her purse. As she drops a few coins into the box, she again looks at the young man's face. She has not spoken a word. The boy does not speak either, but he smiles at her, his eyes looking deep into hers. She feels her heart starting to beat wildly. She feels she is blushing, and lowers her eyes. Her friends are following her example: they too are dropping coins into the box. The young man thanks them politely and is already turning towards another group of girls who are laughing loudly. Noriko and her friends proceed towards the building where they have a class in French literature. 'Kawaii!'[22] All Noriko's girl-friends are of the same opinion. She looks straight ahead.

'Noriko, what about you? Don't you think he's cute?'

'He's a third-year student. . . . I've seen him before at a meeting of Amnesty International.'

'Isn't he good-looking!'

'Noriko, don't you think he's very cute?'

It is Mariko who repeats her question, addressing Noriko. Now, having walked a step or two ahead of the group, she turns round and finds herself almost face to face with Mariko.

'Yes, he's really very cute.'

She answers like someone waking from a long day-dream. Like someone who has been dreaming with eyes open.

Mariko goes on: 'And d'you know what? He looked at you in a strange way. . . . I think he likes you. . . .'

---

[22] Kawaii: pretty, cute, nice – a favourite word of young girls.

Noriko's three classmates begin to giggle. Noriko feels awkward and doesn't know what to say. So she starts to giggle also. . . .

That evening she remembers how difficult it had been for her to get to sleep. She had seen the young man again, and it was true – he liked her. He had gone out of his way to invite her to have a coffee, then another, then another. . . .

She sees again, as if it were yesterday, that first date. That first date, so long awaited, so dreaded. She was sitting facing him. In that '*nomiya*' patronized by students. Among the rowdy, disorderly groups the two of them seemed a little anachronistic.

It is the first time he has invited her to dinner. It is the first time she is eating in the company of a man, without the protective cover of her classmates. She is listening to him. He seems quite at ease. He talks as almost always of great concepts, humanitarian actions. He gets carried away a little, as always. He is so different from the others. She drinks in his words. She drowns in his beautiful eyes. She feels herself a woman at last, a real woman who wants to get close to her man, who wants to become one body with him. She knows he is going to suggest that she goes home with him. She knows she will accept. She knows she is going to encounter something they call happiness.

Hitoshi has just finished his *miso* soup; raising his bowl to his lips, he uses his chopsticks to help the remaining bits of seaweed and vegetables sticking to the bottom slide into his mouth. Above the red lacquer of the bowl his eyes are on his mother, who has not yet touched her cup of tea. She should now be starting her interrogation, but she wants to go on day-dreaming. All those images from the past seem to put a smile in her heart. They also help her to understand.

Hitoshi makes a point of finishing off the few bits of crumb-fried hamburger scattered on the remains of the rice, all of whose grains are now a rosy pink.

Noriko again lets her memory drift back to those months in her life which, she realizes, formed the only really passionate moments she has ever known. Those days spent waiting for him, those nights spent loving one another. That great inner hollow in which everything takes on profounder resonances. That great hollow in which she had sometimes let herself be carried away like a veritable walnut shell in a maelstrom. A whirlwind of emotions. She re-emerged as if drenched in desire and voluptuous longings. She sees again all those shared, delicious moments. Nothing else existed. All around them there was non-existence, non-importance, nothingness . . .

'Gochisō sama deshita.'[23]

Her big son extracts his long limbs from under the little table where he had kept them crossed, and unwinds his tall body. He goes to the fridge where he takes a second bottle of Coca-Cola which he will drink while he is studying. He slowly ascends the narrow, steep little stair, towards his desk.

Noriko also stands up and, in her turn, climbs the carpeted stairs.

Noriko has been doing a lot of thinking. Her son's emotional growing pains have forced her to rediscover in the remotest corners of her memory sensations, emotions she had long forgotten. Which she had buried under piles of life's daily this and that. Reason. Be reasonable. Sensible. Enter the prison cell awaiting you. Do what they all expect of you. Comfort. Her handsome revolutionary had left her . . . for he had to leave her one day, she knew that

---

[23] Formal phrase of thanks after a meal, accompanied by a slight bow.

from the start. He was not a part of the common order of things. He needed none of that. But she had stayed with it, along with all the others. With her sisters in equality. At first she had refused to accept. No, she would show she was different. She would not be like the rest of them. She would wait for him. She would be the companion of his adventures. She would wait until he came down from the heights to more accessible spheres. . . . She would try to understand. She would understand. . . . But life, with its wretched little tricks to make us do what we do not want to do, life, inexorably, had begun to wear down her resistance, had gone to work on her, as we say. It is so difficult to put up a fight all the time, never to drop one's guard. It is so comfortable to let oneself float with the current. We are told that in any case the current will bear us along to calm waters, to peaceful banks on which the grass grows rich and soft. So then one begins to allow oneself to be carried away a little, to take it easy, to get one's breath back. After that, it is more and more difficult to swim against the current again, to fight.

So Noriko had ended up, towards the age of twenty-six accepting to meet a respectable man with a fine future before him, and whose merits were sung by her mother. Big company. Responsible post. Serious. He was eight years older than Noriko. He wasn't ugly, he wasn't good-looking either. He was very nice, especially at the beginning. They married, and Noriko began to build up her household. Little household troubles. Little satisfactions, for the most part material, financial. Two years after her wedding, Noriko was pregnant.

When Noriko gave birth to Hitoshi, she understood that he would be *her* child, that he would probably be the only one, that he would become what was most important in her life. When, at the end of several days, the hospital staff allowed her to hold the little creature in her arms, against her body, she understood the importance of that life, curled close against her flesh, and she decided there had never been and would never be anything more essential to her than this child. So she dedicated herself entirely to this child, who soon occupied all the available space in her heart and in her mind.

Her husband who, she now realized, had never meant much to her, became more and more a kind of stranger living in her house, seeing to the material side of things in exchange for a home he could come to and find a bit of human warmth. That warmth which, symbolically, penetrated every dilated pore of his being when he plunged, after a long day at the office, followed by a long evening drinking, into that *ofuro*[24] which Noriko maintained at the correct temperature until he returned to the family fold. When, after shedding his clothes, he let himself sink slowly into that burning bath, when in the tiny cubical bath, knees up to his chin, he let that delicious, violent heat penetrate to the marrow of his bones. That warmth was also what she gave him by the presence of her body awaiting him on the futon spread on the tatami.

For a long time little Hitoshi had slept between his father and mother. The first years of his life had been passed, physically, between the two of them. Little Hitoshi could not imagine any other place. Nor could Noriko. Yet, ever since he had been installed in his own room, she had rediscovered sufficient feeling for this man who shared her bed, her *ofuro*, her life, sufficient feeling to allow her to 'relieve' him from time to time. 'Relieve' was always the word she thought of to describe this sexual servicing. He would sometimes come home totally exhausted and would fall asleep almost even in the *ofuro*.

---

[24] *Ofuro*: traditional Japanese bath.

Other evenings he would get worked up again, and she considered it her duty to give him satisfaction. Not all the time, but from time to time. . . . She thought it was necessary for the healthy equilibrium of their married life, therefore necessary for her son's healthy equilibrium too. On those evenings, instead of presenting him with a frigid, stubborn back, she would turn towards him and set to work 'relieving' him. In order to achieve her ends, she employed the methods or rather the one method she had found most expeditious, and so the most satisfactory for her. He himself, apparently, seemed to be satisfied by this method. 'Relieved'. Yes, it was with a true sigh of relief that he would turn over a few minutes later and start to snore. Everybody was content.

That evening she has just 'serviced' or 'relieved' her husband, and, as usual, while he snores beside her, she stays lying on her back, her eyes wide open on the chink of light filtering through the curtains that do not quite meet. The ray of light comes from the street lamp, and inscribes a geometrical figure on the ceiling, varying very little from night to night, and looking rather like a little star. Noriko watches her star and starts thinking. Thinking, thinking. It seems as if she will spend all her life thinking. Going over in her mind all the problems, the solutions, the plans, the projects, the hopes, the fears, the terrors. . . .

She is gradually losing her son. He is escaping her control. He is calling into question the attraction of the 'prestigious university'. He has discovered something more important, more pressing. She guesses he is devoured by an internal fire. His mind is in a turmoil. If the lid is not lifted off the boiling pot, he will explode, her son. She senses he is at the end of his tether. He will never make it. The entrance examination is drawing near, but he seems to be removing himself from it, further and further.

Noriko imagines all kinds of ways out. The one way to

bring him back to his studies is to give him sexual satisfaction. To satisfy his frustrated sexual urge. If she allows him to approach a girl of his own age, the fat will be in the fire. He will never be able to handle the situation. He will not know the best way to go about it. He will have to start playing a cat-and-mouse game. She cannot imagine him wasting his time in that way, wasting his energy running after sweet little things who, certainly, will lead him a fine dance. . . .

For an instant she wonders if she should seek the services of a professional. But the idea is brushed aside as soon as envisaged. How could she let her son be seduced in that way? How could she give him that kind of sexual start in life? She who has taken care of the smallest detail, who has always protected him, can she send him out into the thick of the sexual fray like that, empty-handed, defenceless, with only his naïvety as a shield? No, no! She is not going to sacrifice a whole structure of care, counsels, preparations, on such a chancy throw of the dice.

Her general's mind keeps revolving its strategies. Comes up against blank walls. Returns to the starting-point. Looks at the problem from another angle. The problem: she has to act quickly, before everything is wrecked, her son's life, her own life, everything. . . . The solution: unknown.

Who can rescue him? . . . Who else but herself? . . . Has she not always done everything for his well-being? Has she not always helped him whenever he has needed her? Has she not always smoothed his path in life for him? She bore him in pain. She has sacrificed her life to him . . . her whole life. All her hopes . . . her reason for living. She had promised herself, very long ago, to do everything to help make him succeed in what she had decided he would succeed in doing. Everything. . . . Do everything. . . . And now she is at a loss because her son needs to be 'serviced', to be 'relieved'. The word switches on in her mind a series of flashes, winking lights, clockworks. The images are like those used to demonstrate exactly what has happened in a traffic accident. An enormous danger. Blinding flashes. 'Relieved'. She relieves her husband, doesn't she, a man she does not love? A man who means nothing to her. Her son represents everything. And, besides, she *is* her son.

At present, all seems clear to her. Calm. The feeling of peace following an intense struggle. The little star is still shining on the grey ceiling. But Noriko does not have to look at it any longer now. She no longer needs to gaze at it while following her trains of thought. Her son is saved! . . . And it will be she alone who has saved him! . . .

ALL FOR MY CHILD . . . OR NORIKO.

The Contract

The sinuous perfection of line, the arch of the back, the fullness of the sumptuous crupper, the loaded breasts delirious in their velvety swayings. The black suspender belt cuts in two this majestic body and seems to increase its fullness. The narrow bands of black elastic running down the haunches underline their swelling curves. The girl sways, the curve becomes more pronounced, the waist tenses, the black stockings rise very high on the broad white thighs. The white thighs against the dark border of the stocking. . . .

'Hai dozo.'[25]

Tanaka raises haggard eyes from the document he is supposed to be examining. The young girl holding out his cup of tea is small and skinny.

---

[25] 'Hai dozo': 'Come in.'

'Domo arigato gozaimasu.'[26] The young girl smiles and uncovers a row of enormous teeth, encased in two snaggle teeth that are even larger. Most of his colleagues think they are a supreme refinement – 'charm points', they are called. He gazes sombrely after the narrow hips. The legs are made to look shorter by woolly socks rising to mid-calf. Under the socks, tights. In her office slippers she has a slightly duck-toed walk.

Tanaka closes his eyes again but is unable to pick up the thread of his marvellous day-dream. This evening he will go to Kabukicho[27] to get another eyeful . . . of dreams. . . .

Anyhow, why is he haunted by these obsessive images of unreal and inaccessible women – inaccessible at least to him, Tanaka, for the moment. One day, perhaps. . . .

As far back as he can remember, his present fantasies were unleashed by the apparition of Ursula Andress on the immense movie screen. She was walking slowly out of the ocean which created a royal blue backdrop for her statuesque body. Her breasts were streaming with thousands of water droplets and had the colour of freshly melted gold. Tanaka had his first willed erection. He must have been nine or ten years old. . . .

'Not this evening. I have some work to finish.' The three young men looking in on him and laughing all come from the same mould – well-cut suits, the grey of whose fabric is shot with another tone but remains inalterably grey and 'elegant'. Like Tanaka, they have been working in the company for about a year. Almost every evening they feel obliged to go and drink sake or beer in a *nomiya*, nibbling little snacks of fried fish or stewed octopus.

---

[26] 'Domo arigato gozaimasu.': 'Thank you very much.' Formal expression of thanks.

[27] Kabukicho: Tokyo entertainment district in Shinjuku.

Tanaka had often taken part in their outings but had been bored stiff by them. There were never any women, or if by chance two or three were included in the group, they were always so-called 'good' girls, prim and proper, completely lacking in sex appeal.

As he clears away the things on his desk, Tanaka plans his evening's programme. First of all the Italian restaurant in the basement of the building. At least once a week he likes to go to this place smelling of garlic and tomato sauce. On each little table, on a blood-red table-cloth, a real candle burns. Their patches of yellow light illumine the obscurity of the little room. The waiters know him and try to give him his favourite table. Once installed in his corner, he has the feeling of being able to see without being seen. Many young couples. For the most part people of twenty-five, twenty-six years of age, but who look eighteen. The girl drinks very little, being afraid to lose control of herself. The boy downs too much red wine, to which he is not accustomed, and his face, under the candlelight, takes on the brick-red colour of a ski instructor's weathered skin. From time to time foreigners come to disturb the peaceful atmosphere of the little restaurant. Tanaka had been able to admire magnificent creatures with manes of blonde hair and generously low-cut dresses.

The foreigners always created a kind of panic, talking and laughing too loudly, trying to explain to the bewildered waiter incomprehensible orders, changes in the menu. Tanaka was amused by these outbursts as he sat calmly sipping his bottle of red wine, which had been served with his spaghetti. The owner's cellar was reasonably good and inexpensive, and Tanaka never failed to finish a whole bottle. When he gets up from his table, his blood is warmed and his head filled with fantasies, each more carnal than the last.

Tanaka gets up from his little corner table, takes the bill

that is in a sort of metal cup and moves towards the cash desk.

'Domo arigato gozaimasu,' the cashier says, handing him his change and rewarding him with a broad smile. Tanaka stumbles slightly on the first step; he is feeling great. The gust of fresh air that greets him as he leaves the restaurant makes him feel even better. With a firm, steady step he makes for the Kabukicho. In fact he has only to cross the broad Shinjuku avenue and he finds himself in a universe of pastel-pink neon, the din of conflicting musical offerings, touts in gaudy costumes.

Woman is everywhere, woman for sale. *Peep-show*, *Pink Salon*, *Striptease*, *Hostess Bar*, *Massage*, *Sauna*. An entire universe of tits and ass. Open mouths, enticing looks. Between the different neon signs, idlers gawping and small-time sellers of sex, many of them with almost shaven scalps in the local gangster or *yakuza* style. Very few women to be seen. You have to pay to see them. They are inside, waiting for clients.

Tanaka knows exactly where he is going. For him, massages, saunas, 'special services', etc. etc., are no longer of any interest. He has tried everything, more or less. The peep-shows with their 'finger service' had interested him for a while. The girl not only exhibited herself in her cage of two-way mirrors, but in addition, for the price of a ticket handed to her through a little trapdoor, would come and 'finish off' through that same little trapdoor the erection she had aroused. Those fingers, cold or warm – strangers' fingers. The girl's expressionless face on the other side of the mirror, just a few inches from his own face. Yes, he had had his 'peep-show period', but the satisfaction he had derived from it had never been complete. Doubtless because all the girls were Japanese, Koreans or Filipinas, all Asiatics, his own family as it were, like his sisters almost. He could never discover in those plump little juvenile bodies the essence of his fantasies. No, what he required were big, slender creatures, wild mares, blonde manes flying in the wind, powerful cruppers, rippling muscles under a pale skin that shuddered nervously, like a savage beast's. . . .

The New Theatre of Shinjuku always employed foreigners. They generally came on at the end of the show, the after-dinner mint, the ultimate pleasure. . . . A discreet entrance, a little elevator, third floor. On the second floor a small karaoke club where half-stewed 'salarymen' came to show off their execrable singing talents.

The doors of the elevator open on two or three hilarious flushed faces with brilliant eyes. 'Up or down?' Tanaka simply points upwards. 'Oh! we. . . .' They all three point their fingers downwards and at the same time burst out laughing. As the doors are closing Tanaka hears one of them whispering to the other two: 'Third floor!' A fresh outburst of drunken laughter that dies away as the elevator descends to the basement.

The doors open on reddish lighting and a cosy odour of worn carpet and stale cigarettes. The ticket office notice says 2,000 yen on weekdays, 2,500 on Saturday evenings. Tanaka hands two tickets to the half-pint with the wrinkled face who mutters something. The entrance hall is big, something like an old cinema's. In one corner a kiosk selling candy, popcorn and non-alcoholic drinks. On all the walls gigantic posters of porno magazine strippers . . . provocatively thrust-out knockers, stretched cheeks, lubricious lips and languorous, come-hither eyes. Their foreign flesh is a creamy golden colour, or porky pink. Tanaka takes it all in. He knows those posters by heart, and certain of the paper dolls are already part of Tanaka's fantasies. He buys a Coke and a packet of Mild Seven. He pushes open one of the three heavy doors, also padded with old carpet. The humidity, the smoke and the palpable heat of the interior. The heavy door closes behind him with a dull thud. Tanaka stands leaning against the wall until his eyes get used to the darkness. The place is circular, quite vast, with a high ceiling. Rows of small seats around a circular stage which is connected to a larger one in the middle of the room.

Between the two platforms a sort of promenade or catwalk carpeted in pale beige. Just like the circular stage. Those spectators in the first row have their noses on a level with the stage. There is not one vacant seat in the first row. There is a dense crowd, with only one or two empty seats further back. For a while Tanaka gazes at all those napes tense with expectation, attention, concentration. There is music but no talking, no laughter. The men seem very solemn: sex is serious business. All those heads are turned reverently towards the ceremony taking place before their very eyes. A sacrifice of flesh. The girl lying posed on the edge of the centre stage is rotating slowly with it, like a wooden horse on a children's merry-go-round. From time to time the mechanism, probably not oiled sufficiently, makes her flesh quiver a little. She is illuminated by a powerful spotlight coming from a glazed panel high up on the ceiling. In its chalky-white rays enormous spirals of smoke swirl lazily. A sort of volatile fluff, sensual also.

A burst of applause rouses Tanaka from his contemplative communion. The girl waves and collects the various props she has used during her number. She casts a glance at the glass box and, apparently obedient to some kind of signal, waves her gracious hand invitingly towards the public. At once three men jump up together and begin to do a frantic *jan-ken-pon*[28] like little boys to decide a winner.

---

[28] *Jan-ken-pon*: scissors, paper, stone – a counting-out game.

The latter raises his arms like a boxer greeting his fans. He is fairly young, not yet thirty. He is wearing a pearl-grey suit but he has loosened his awful striped tie. Beaming all over his flushed face, he climbs on to the centre stage, encouraged by the applause that now breaks out even more wildly. He lies down, makes himself comfortable, closes his eyes, trying to relax for the pleasure to come. He has removed his jacket, folded it neatly and laid it on the beige carpeting not far from where he lies. The jacket starts rotating at the same time as his body, and the girl advances. . . .

Lina scrutinizes her face in the mirror and freshens her lipstick. The brilliant scarlet glitters in the crude lighting of the cramped dressing-room. Beside her, two strippers are chattering in their incomprehensible language. Though she doesn't understand one word of their anecdotes, she senses the crudity of the expressions. Their voices are harsh and the 'r' is rolled endlessly. Their laughter is oily and coarse. A far cry from the refined speech of the geisha. The two girls are smoking cigarette after cigarette and the air of the little room is getting thicker and thicker.

When she first arrived here, Lina wondered how her fellow-troupers would welcome her. It's always difficult when you're new. And a foreigner at that. She had been dumped in this country at the world's end but which offered a fabulous contract. Joe, the guy who had recruited her, had explained everything to her, what would happen, for whom she would be working, what she would have to do. When he had made a request for her to come and sit at his table after her number, naturally she had thought he was going to make a pass at her. But immediately he had started talking about the 'contract', the conditions of work. This guy simply proposed she should leave the rotten dump in which she was working her ass off, say 'fuck you' to the big Mexican pig exploiting her, take a jet to Tokyo and be able to pay the fees for Jimmy's private school.

All she would have to do was more or less what she'd already been doing for the past four years. The only difference would be that she wouldn't be stripping in a low dive full of half-crocked lushes but in a kind of theatre, and that she would have to invite men on the stage. Naturally she jibbed at that – hand jobs in public! – but Joe had calmly explained that in Japan there was no risk whatsoever, that they never had any problems! That the men behaved themselves. He had also made clear what hygienic precautions were taken. Lina had told him to come back next day and she would give him her answer. But when she got up from the table she already knew she would say yes.

It was a fabulous offer and she really needed a change of air. And she had made a change of air with a vengeance! She had prepared for the journey like any other tourist; she had bought guides to Japan and to Tokyo, as well as a handbook of elementary conversational phrases which she had tried in vain to memorize.

On her arrival at Narita, Joe had introduced her to his bosses who had come in a huge limousine as white as their dazzling suits. They were both wearing dark glasses and Lina remembered how she had been impressed by those two short guys who gave off such an aura of power. They had dealt with the matter in a businesslike way that left nothing to chance. Joe translated. She had agreed. She could not take her eyes off the left hand of one of the men. The tip of the little finger was missing. Joe had explained to her later that when he was younger his boss had failed in his duty towards one of his chiefs. As an apology, he had cut off the end of his little finger with a kitchen knife. Joe, smiling, had told her this was common practice among the *yakuzas* and that it was a way of reducing errors.

Then she had met the two girls who now were busy laughing their heads off on their stools, their eyes full of tears, choking on the smoke of their cigarettes. Lina turns towards them with a smile on her lips. Their laughter is infectious. They have passed a kimono over their stage costume – or rather their lack of stage costume. The open dressing-gowns reveal their mesh stockings. One has white ones, the other black. Their thighs are too skinny for mesh stockings, Lina thinks, smiling all the while. The girls have kicked off their high heels and put on slippers, which give them a grotesque aspect.

Tanaka looks at his feet that pound the hard grey asphalt with the regularity of a metronome. His shoes could do with a good spit and polish. But that is only a brief passing thought. In fact he is trying to relive in the moviehouse of his mind the images he has recorded this evening. The show was the apotheosis of his fantasies. When he had seen that superb creature advancing down the catwalk, he had understood that his dreams could become reality. The loudspeakers had announced 'Lina the Stripteaser', who had arrived straight from Las Vegas. Like all the other men around him, Tanaka had let out a soft 'Oh!' of respectful exclamation. The girl on her spike heels appeared like a giantess, her black stockings sheathing long, solid but beautifully tapering legs. The divine pair of cheeks seemed even more enticing with their border of black lace decorating a sort of corset imprisoning her waist and exaggerating the rounded hips. Breasts huge, spherical like those on the girls in porno comics. The place was quietly excited. Tanaka pressed himself back against the wall. His face set, tense and almost doleful. Like an archaeologist confronted with a mummy, the reward for years of effort. . . .

Yes, the young woman he had seen this evening was so perfect for him that he had the feeling she had emerged directly from his imagination, that he had created her, that she belonged to him.

Staring at the tips of his shoes as they bring him towards the station, Tanaka is pondering the best way to get his hands on his property.

The following days see Tanaka preparing to bring off his coup. He is fully aware of the difficulties, the enormous difficulties he will encounter. Even just to get near Lina. How can he separate her from her bosses, the *yakuzas*, or her boy-friend, her protector or whoever? How can he get her to notice him? How can he get her to meet him? How to make her his very own? Yes, Tanaka is perfectly conscious of the hugeness of the task, but, on the other hand, he knows that nothing can stop him from attaining his object. It is simply a question of time and energy, but in the last analysis he cannot imagine any other outcome than the one indicated by destiny. The vibrations he had felt in his body and in his very soul signified something too strong and too profound to brook impediment. When one has had a revelation such as Tanaka had had this evening, one simply cannot envisage defeat. Others are struck by artistic, humanitarian, moral revelations, others receive mystic revelations. But Tanaka has found his art, his religion in the body of that woman, in that flesh, in those curves. Some may call the nature of Tanaka's revelation crude and vulgar. Some may talk of man's lower instincts, of bestiality. Others may not want to think about such things. Yet for Tanaka such questions do not exist. He reacts like a man who has suddenly found his vocation. Nothing at all can stop him. Vocations are neither noble nor unworthy. Vocations urge a man in certain directions, make him take tortuous paths, roads upon which only a strongly motivated man can set foot. Soon, vocation gives way to motivation. Motivation is the fuel of life. Without fuel, the stove goes out and turns cold.

Lina opens her eyes, then shuts them again immediately. Although the heavy curtains are closed, the light filters through and gives the tiny room a greyish illumination. Deafening, the roar of traffic running down below. From time to time a horn's lively toot rips through that incessant rumbling. Lina turns over on her stomach, and, slipping both arms under the pillow, tries to find a cool spot. It must be nearly four in the afternoon; her alarm clock will soon start to ring. She opens her eyes again and this time lets them wander round the room that has now become so familiar.

Her clothes are tumbled on the one armchair in the room. One black stocking hangs lifelessly from one of the arm-rests. On the carpeted floor a stiletto-heeled shoe is lying on its side, looking like a wounded beast. She has been here for three weeks. Sometimes she feels as if she arrived only yesterday, at other times the three weeks weigh upon her like an eternity. She sinks to the hollow of the wave, on the verge of throwing up.

Sometimes when she is on-stage she feels like a queen. All those greedy eyes devouring every inch of her body, all those hands stretching out to touch her, feel her. Sometimes all she feels is a profound disgust, a nausea rising from the very bowels of her being and almost suffocating her. Sometimes she has to get a grip of herself again, of body and soul, in order to be able to breathe normally once more. She opens her mouth and, breathing in deeply, takes great gulps of air. A fish out of water. She has no friends. Not really. She knows a lot of people but she feels a longing to call up someone, to hear a friendly voice, a familiar, reassuring voice. But there is no one on her heart's wavelength. She feels so terribly alone that, were it not for Jimmy, she would chuck in the sponge and take the first plane to anywhere. But where to, actually? And the money? When she had been able to send that big cheque in dollars to the head of Jimmy's school, she had felt so good. Proud of herself. She was going to guarantee the future of that little chap she had been saddled with, big smile and blond shock of hair and everything. He would never want for anything. She would always give him the best in life. And when she had scraped together enough of the moolah to buy herself a nice little bar, she would get a clean, pretty, really OK little house where he can come and live, and he won't be ashamed to invite his friends there.

Very slowly Lina stretches out her right leg and lets it hang over the edge of the mattress, for just a few minutes, without moving. After a while, however, she gets up and sits on the side of the bed. She has a slight hangover. She drank one whisky too many. She smoked too much. Her long fingers ruffling her thick golden hair, she thinks back to last night. . . .

Five in the morning, dawn just breaking, everything looking filthy and grey. Especially in this district, the paradise of nocturnal pleasures. The nocturnal pleasures are now reduced to big piles of black plastic trash-bags. At some street corners there is a small mountain of them disgorging their entrails: trails of long, leftover brown and yellow spaghetti, empty whisky bottles, brightly coloured peelings of fruit or vegetables. Perched on one of these piles a black and grey cat is delicately crunching a magnificent fish-bone. When Lina sees this, she realizes that one doesn't see so many animals roaming freely in these streets. She cannot help stopping at the base of the mountain of trash, and, holding out her fingers to the tiny creature, she murmurs 'puss-puss'. The moggie in question stops chewing to turn on this friendly hand an eye both perplexed and cautious. 'Are you crazy! You'll catch fleas off it.' Joe takes her gently by the elbow and walks along the street with her. The others are now about ten yards ahead of them. 'Hey, Lina, is everything OK? You happy? Tonight on-stage you looked a bit wistful.' He had arrived just before the end of the last show, around four-thirty. At five o'clock the trains started running again, and a lot of spectators stayed there to the end in that muggy, cloying atmosphere, waiting for the first train to take them home. A sort of waiting-room, open all night, sensual and perverse.

That night Lina had had some difficulty in accepting the final *jan-ken-pon* winner. He had greying hair and the pomade with which he had smothered it smelt strong, a sickly, tenacious odour. Lina had almost refused him, but seeing Joe arrive she had not wanted to disappoint or distress him. He had always been so kind to her, so attentive. Beside him she had noticed a fairly young man, dressed like the others in the audience. Physically speaking, nothing out of the ordinary. Yet she could not help looking at his face. There was something strange about him, bizarre, perhaps because he was staring right into her eyes with a singular intensity. It was not the fixed look, the popping eyes that men usually had when gaping at other parts of her body: it was something else. The little grey-haired guy with the perfumed locks who with a broad grin had just dropped his pants, revealing long johns of dubious freshness, brought her back to hard reality.

'If there's anything not as you like it, you must tell me, I'll try to fix things for you. Did you send the money for your kid?'

'Yes, Yuriko came to the post office with me, to give me a hand.'

'You have any problems with the other girls?'

'No.'

'You want to take a day off?'

'No. I need the dough.'

'You'll see, we'll have us a good time at Yamaguchi-san's. He really puts on the Ritz.'

Yamaguchi-san was one of the bosses of the show. Not the top boss whom one almost never met, but the one with whom you did business and who paid on the nail. Lina knew quite well that he was dying to get her into bed, but he did not dare make use of his boss's authority because 'with these foreigners you never know'.

'You know, Yamaguchi-san would very much like to go to bed with you. He asked me if I thought you'd agree.'

'What did you tell him?'

'That you always did just as you pleased.'

'That's correct.'

'The bosses are pleased with you, the takings are going up and it's obvious the majority of patrons come for you.'

'Lina, super star.'

Lina gave a soft laugh. She could not help feeling flattered.

'Wait, I have to buy some fags.'

Lina goes towards the cigarette machine. She is wearing a leather-fringed squaw outfit. The skirt is short, suede, mid-thigh length, also fringed. The boots, mid-calf length, also have fringes. The ensemble is very sexy, and at the same time casual. The beautiful all-American girl, radiant with health, dazzling white teeth and peachy golden skin. Joe watches the fringes swinging on Lina's hips.

'You smoke Japanese cigarettes?'

Lina suddenly swings round. She had not noticed the man in a dark corner untouched by the light of dawn. The man steps forward. She recognizes his eyes. Even more than his eyes, the waves they send out.

'I'm one of your admirers.'

Although his English is a little awkward, the accent is good. The voice a bit too self-conscious, a sort of Japanese Humphrey Bogart. He is shorter than Lina. He is looking up at her.

'Who's he?'

Yuriko had turned round and had shouted in her nasal American-English accent.

'One of my fans.'

'Bring him along, it's my birthday.'

Yuriko bursts out laughing and takes Yamaguchi's arm, leaning heavily on him: she is already quite drunk.

Joe comes up.

'What's the matter?'

'Nothing,' Lina says. 'He's with us.'

The party had been bizarre indeed. First of all a party that begins at five in the morning. . . . Yuriko was soon legless and had begun to strip. Professional reflex perhaps. Her voice was getting hoarser and hoarser. And the 'r' was rolled more richly than ever. The men smiled at her rather faded body. As if hesitating what attitude to take towards Yuriko's provocative words and gestures. To get into the mood of things, they were drinking whisky after whisky.

Yamaguchi's apartment was in a high-class respectable building, with a huge entrance hall luxuriously carpeted, and a guard behind a small window. There was a fairly spacious living-room and a somewhat cramped bedroom. Yamaguchi had laid down red carpeting everywhere and the room was lit by crude white neon tubes. This décor suggested a tit-and-ass magazine on a small budget. Lina could not enter into the spirit of things and, like the men, started knocking back whisky. From time to time she stole glances at the man she had picked up in the street, and smiled at him. He was smiling also, his eyes were radiant. Yuriko had perched on Joe's knees and started to undress him. Joe tried to resist, pretenting to be a virgin. Yuriko kept repeating in her whisky-sodden croak: 'Yuriko no tanjobi da kara.'[29] It was her birthday, no one could refuse her anything. The man had placed himself discreetly in a corner, a little apart. Lina smiled at him again and, patting the sofa, signalled to him to come and sit beside her.

Tanaka is bent over the list of figures with which the little tea-serving secretary with the duck-toed walk has just presented him. He casts a furtive glance at his wrist-watch. Just another half-hour and he will be able to escape into Lina's world. The very thought of it arouses in him a rising wave of sensuality which is playing delicious tricks with his spinal cord and rises in a voluptuous shiver all along his backbone.

It had happened last night, at last, after many nights spent watching her along with other men; last night, or rather this morning. Today was Saturday so he would work only until one o'clock. He had come straight to the office at nine o'clock. No sleep, but what did that matter! He had carried out successfully the first step in his project. He had almost touched Lina, he had brushed against her, he had breathed her perfume, smelt her breath, as unbelievable as that might seem. Lina had appeared to be interested in him. But, after all, why should it be unbelievable? Had he not decided that it would happen thus, right from the start? In fact she had been so indifferent to the make-believe orgy going on all round them that she had given him all her attention, telling him of the difficulties of her life in Japan. Tanaka had listened religiously to all she said. Once or twice the others had tried to break in upon their

[29] 'Yuriko no tanjobi da kara': 'Because it's Yuriko's birthday.'

intimacy, but in vain, and had not seemed too put out by it. On the other hand, the rictus disfiguring Yamaguchi's lower face – she had accorded him only a few scraps of attention – had got worse as the evening went on. Tanaka had taken an instant dislike to him, this Yamaguchi, and his heart had leapt with joy when he noticed that Lina felt the same way towards the man.

Tanaka gives himself an instant replay of his meeting with Lina. She is beautiful, at ease. Her long golden legs are crossed in front of her, and the fact that the sofa is rather low gives them an enthralling dimension. The suede leather miniskirt covers rather less than half her thigh. In her left hand she has a big glass of whisky which she rests on her knee. She shakes it slightly, the ice-cubes clink in the golden-brown liquid, and it reminds Tanaka of a television ad. In the fingers of her other hand she is holding a long English cigarette, from which she takes regular long drags that she blows out almost immediately, with a charming pout that makes her very full lips even more sensual. Tanaka cannot take his eyes off this creature who represents everything he has ever desired. Everything his body has always thirsted for, thirsted to suffer for. Just a few inches away from him sits the realization of his wildest, most passionate dreams. Tanaka advances prudently, so that this dream will not disappear in a puff of smoke, as from a magic wand. He has to use all the skills of a bomb-disposal expert in order to get what he wants. He does not want the bomb to go off in his hands. A too sudden movement and everything would be blown to smithereens, shattered, volatilized. He was lucky enough to stumble upon this treasure: he does not want to send it to kingdom come through stupid haste. Now, he has all the time in the world.

Lina puts down her cup of coffee and takes another cigarette out of the gilded cigarette-case. She screws it into a sort of cigarette-holder which is supposed to filter out all the poisonous elements of the tobacco. She also likes the pose it makes her assume. She does not venture to use the long, black, gilded cigarette-holder of the thirties stars, so she has found this alternative.

The zealous young waiter, his ears crimson, changes the ashtray in which lies her last cigarette-end. It is one of those days when she feels at the top of her form. There's radiant sunshine: on the café terrace, one of the few Tokyo pavement terraces, young men in T-shirts instinctively turn their faces towards the sun's gentle warmth. A few tables away some foreigners are sitting. Good-looking young men who seem to have come straight out of a James Dean movie. Models. From time to time one or the other of them turns towards Lina. Her beauty is too provocative and too fleshy for her to be one of their calling. Yet they cannot help looking sideways towards this big blonde girl. Perhaps they do not know how to approach her. Lina dismisses the boys from her mind, in order to enjoy to the full this sunny day. Tonight she doesn't start work until nine, and she has all the end of the afternoon and the early evening to herself. Well, almost, because her little office worker is coming to join her soon. She lets her thoughts drift back to that man whose gaze is so intense and whose attitude seems so bizarre. The way he had accosted her. He had told her everything. How he had come to watch her every evening he was free. How he had manoeuvred a meeting with her. What it meant to him to be with her. All this delivered with such calm sang-froid, such restraint. His English was a little hesitant and often he was at a loss for words, but she knew that even if he had spoken in his own tongue he would not have talked faster or said any more. He gave the impression of a man who knows exactly where he is going, who knows he will get what he wants. He also explained to her how important she, Lina, was to him, that she was the source of his inspiration, that she could not comprehend all at once just how much she meant to him, but that he would gradually explain everything, that the future now belonged to them. Yes, she couldn't help feeling fascinated by that little chap. There was something mystical about him that disturbed and at the same time excited her. He, on the other hand, seemed to want to control his excitement. Nevertheless, the things he whispered in her ear, so calmly, were full of sensuality, but it was as if he had deliberately put a lid on that sensuality, and that he would lift it off only when everything was ready. Until then he seemed as if he did not want to touch her or even look at her. Except for a few furtive, careful glances . . .

'It's warm, isn't it?'

He's there, standing in front of her. She raises her eyes to his but is dazzled by the sun that glitters richly on the man's hair. His face remains in shadow. She cannot make out his features. Only the silver frame of his glasses seems white in the black hole of his face.

'Sit down,' Lina says, indicating the second chair at the table.

As he sits down, his face is revealed. He is smiling. His eyes are looking right into hers. . . . She is smiling at him also.

'It was great last night . . . this morning, rather. . . . I slept until three o'clock. I had such a hangover. . . . I drank too much.'

Every time she used some unusual expression, she gave him a literal paraphrase. Yet he seemed to understand everything she said. He had watched many American movies, he had told her.

'I had to go to work. I did not sleep. Well, a little . . .

with open eyes. . . .'

Lina looks at Tanaka, who is smiling sweetly. She cannot see in his face any traces of the fatigue a night on the tiles should have left on it. For a fraction of a second he frightens her a little.

'I know a little Italian restaurant. Do you like Italian cooking? . . .'

'Why do you do this kind of thing?'

The question all the men in her life have asked her. As if one would ask a station employee why he did his job. He could always reply that it was because he liked trains.

'Because I like men.'

'But at that place they are no longer men?'

'Yes, you're right, I don't consider them men. They turn into objects who look upon me as an object. But after all, if I didn't like men, I couldn't do it. Why? Does it upset you?'

'No! Yes and no! Sometimes it even excites me to think of all those. . . . At other times, I get hopping mad. . . . It's strange. . . . What were the reactions of the men in your life? I mean. . . .'

Lina stretches out an arm to the shelf behind her. As she does so, one of her white breasts stretches and points upwards. Tanaka cannot resist it, takes it in his hand, then in his mouth. Lina, bringing her arm back in front of her, finds the man crushing his mouth on her breast and gently caresses his hair. Then she digs a cigarette out of the packet, lights it, hands it to Tanaka, lights herself another. For a few moments they both smoke in silence, watching the whorls of smoke rising to the ceiling and spreading there. Tanaka's head is resting on Lina's breast, just above the left nipple. The man looks so small.

'The men in my life? . . . A lot. . . . Not many who

meant anything to me. . . . At first . . . it excites them, the things I do. . . . It upsets all their sacred taboos. . . . But after a while either it disgusts them or it makes them jealous, sick with jealousy. In the end, they take themselves off . . . or I do. . . . You . . .'

'I've told you I'll explain it all gradually. You can't understand everything straight away. You must completely convince yourself that you were made for me, and that you can only belong to me . . . and I am yours.'

Lina sits up to kiss his forehead and takes the opportunity to flick the ash from her cigarette into the ashtray on the shelf.

'You see, you don't understand . . .'

Lina turns to protest, but Tanaka lays a finger on her lips.

'And that's quite normal!'

'Why?' Lina manages to get out, despite the forefinger Tanaka has laid on her mouth.

Tanaka smiles at her. He has a diabolical look . . . just a little . . .

'You want another whisky?'

Lina is already getting up to go to the little table where the ice-bucket and the already opened bottle are waiting. She has kept her black stockings on, and Tanaka says nothing.

Weeks, months pass by. Little by little Lina and Tanaka get to know each other. He gives her the satisfaction of feeling indispensable, primordial. She finds peace of mind in satisfying the wildest desires of this little man. Of this slightly diabolical child, who is so lovable. This human being who, without complexes, forces himself to play out his fantasies to the very end. Lina sometimes feels she is the creator of a scenario that has been rehearsed many times. She who has known more men than she can remember realizes that she has never really let herself go, never plumbed the utmost depths of her being. Her body becomes a complicated instrument dedicated to creating or destroying.

He for his part stages all his accumulated dreams. He is bathed in an almost permanent state of exaltation. He too attains a beneficent equilibrium, a calm. Yet this optimal state is often on the verge of madness.

After three months of this kind of existence Lina begins to think about it all. All she remembers of these weeks is a uniform continuity of time bathed in sex and sensuality. There is practically no difference between the theatre spectacle and the bed with Tanaka – his bed. For they are using his hotel room, which is becoming more and more sordid. Familiar objects in it take on a smell, a colour that sometimes make her feel sick. She is drinking more and more, smoking as much as ever. Often she finds herself thinking about the life she is leading. She is beginning to feel worn out, too much used. She has a dream that keeps coming back to haunt her nights:

She is lying down, resting in a sort of warm, sticky jelly: her body is floating in this stuff. She feels something like a slight burn on her breast, and when she puts her hand there she pulls off with a cry of horror a whitish leech. In fact her whole body is covered with them. The little beasts are all over her breasts and thighs, in the folds of her flesh. . . . She shouts, and her horror increases when she sees the head of one of the things. It has a man's grimacing, ugly face, with reptilian teeth, evil eyes. Usually that is when she wakes up.

'Lina super star.' The man, obviously drunk as a pig, has difficulty in keeping upright. He suddenly appeared before them, from among a group of revellers occupying the small private tatami room in the restaurant. It is a *sushiya*,[30] which consists simply of a row of stools lined up against a wooden counter. The three youths behind the counter are wearing round their cropped heads tightly rolled towels. They all three have short hair, cut in brush style. Their headgear makes them look a bit like pirates. They are distributing little slices of raw fish which they slice up with magical dexterity, using their big, sharp knives.

The drunk has left the group in the inner tatami room which is situated behind the backs of the people sitting on the stools. Eyes shining, almost weeping, he has greying hair covered with brilliantine. 'You . . . me. . . .' The man makes an indecent gesture. His group of colleagues break into squeals of laughter. Lina does not see them, she only hears them. The other customers at the counter, embarrassed, keep their noses stuck in their bowls of *miso* soup or in their cups of green tea. The pirate cooks seem busier than ever manipulating their huge knives. One of them is engaged in cutting open a small silvery fish which he has just fished out of the aquarium behind him. With the panache of a surgeon, he skilfully slivers the two fillets. The drunk man is insisting noisily: 'Yes . . . we did . . . did it together.' The little fish is still wriggling as it is handed on a minute wooden platter to the gourmet on Lina's right. He delicately takes one of the slivers in his chopsticks, dips it discreetly in his finger-bowl of *shoyu*[31] and raises it to his oily lips. The other half of the fishkin, its bones laid bare, is still feebly wagging its tail. Lina, her napkin to her lips, thrusts away her stool, which falls with a great crash, avoids the grey-haired drunk and dashes towards the door of the toilets.

During that period Lina's depressions increase, become

---

[30] *Sushiya*: a sushi snack-bar, serving mostly raw fish sliced on rolls of vinegared rice.
[31] *Shoyu*: soy sauce (Kikkoman, etc.), made from the soya bean.

permanent. Without mentioning it to Tanaka, she tries to conceive the possibility of a return to the States. . . . Leave this country. . . . Never see that theatre again. . . . One evening, out of curiosity, she climbed into the glass box where Yamaguchi and the guy who does the lighting and the music are sitting. Yamaguchi, slumped in his armchair, torch in hand: it is he who, with signals from his torch through the glass, transmits the order to the girl down on the circular stage to stay there a little longer to service another client or to leave the stage. It's Yuriko on now. Lina lights a cigarette and perches on the window-ledge of the glass box. Her silk kimono falls open on a black-sheathed thigh which, in the position she has taken up, seems even more curvaceous than usual. Yamaguchi's eyes move all the way down her leg, down to the neat black leather shoes, then move back all the way up to Lina's face, gazing down upon him. This guy spends his whole life in an atmosphere of tits and ass and general sexual hanky-panky, yet still finds it possible to get excited, like a dog, by a pair of legs. . . . He starts sweating a bit and leans over, pretending to be interested in the act below. As always, whenever she thinks of him, Lina feels disgust. She also turns towards the stage, which she can see at an angle across his shoulder.

From her cage of glass Lina sees the darkened theatre with the harshly lit revolving stage at its centre. Yuriko's body, thin and pallid, seems spreadeagled as if she were being tortured, broken on the wheel. Her loosened hair on the carpeting frames a face in agony. Her shut eyes are two black streaks. The eyelids heavily sensual. She is rolling her head from left to right and a few hairs are stuck to her sweating cheeks. Her open mouth is groaning with both pleasure and pain.

Lina cannot tear her eyes away from the spectacle of that face. Yet gradually she notices the man crouched beside the naked body. . . . The pale red splotches on Yuriko's flesh. . . . The white collar of the man's shirt cutting a sharp line against the brown nape. . . . The red, lighted candle the man is moving a few inches above Yuriko's skin, the hot red wax dripping. Dozens of napes leaning forward to get the action, share the experience. . . . Dozens of tense napes. . . . Hundreds. . . . Thousands. . . . Lina feels overcome by dizziness. Her eyes cloud over. The image begins to swim slightly before her . . . stops, loses focus again. . . . Like something seen through a microscope with a complicated focusing mechanism . . . making her feel sick.

She tries to be sensible. She has seen worse than that. But she cannot cut the current. Watches all that as one would watch the working of an ant's nest. . . . Withdraw in order not to have them swarming all over one. A sour taste rises to her mouth. She wants to wake up. . . . Another nightmare. Just as she is trying to drag herself away from the sight, from her hypnotized contemplation, she feels a damp hand creeping over her thigh . . . just above the black satin band of her nylon stocking top.

Tanaka is gnawing his pencil, worried. Indeed he is feeling desperate, sensing that Lina is moving away from him, while he refuses to let her go. He is no longer able to convince her that she forms part of his flesh, and though she abandons herself to him from time to time, she remains feverish and strung up. She is afraid. She has told him about her reactions to the work she is doing. Her work that she cannot give up now as she would like to do.

She has talked to him about going back to her own country, but her face suddenly became set, as if she were afraid of his reaction. She is afraid of him. There is something of the hunted beast about him. She can service her 'clients' only at the cost of superhuman efforts, and now she seems to be looking at him, too, as one of her 'clients'. Although she denied it, he himself had formed that disagreeable impression and, when she dismissed it, he had caught in her eyes a flash of terror. How can he restore the confidence she had in him at the start? She will have to get out of her contract with the *yakuzas*. That would appear to be very difficult and she is not doing all that much to secure her freedom. Resignation. Now all day long she wanders the streets of Tokyo, eyes wide, a frightened smile on her lips, her sad lips. Tanaka does not know what to do for the best in order to find again the Lina he knew at the beginning. Why does she want to run away from him? . . .

Lina, like a swimmer out of breath, no longer feels her body but continues to advance inexorably. She must not stop. If she stops she will sink to the bottom, and she knows it. She must go on in order to reach the salvation of the shore, or at least some bit of wreckage she can cling to. Whenever she passes in front of a mirror, she no longer recognizes herself. Oh yes! She recognizes that great Amazon's body, but the features of her face are those of a stranger. That set face, those hunted eyes. . . . How could this have happened to her? . . . She thought she had experienced everything, passed every possible test. . . . Yet suddenly she feels as if eaten up by some inner sickness, something that has quietly insinuated itself into her. Indefinable yet always present. She did not take care and had let herself be overrun by it. She goes on doing whatever they tell her she should do . . . even with Tanaka. . . . She dreads something or other, she does not really know what. Once mistress of herself, of her senses, she has become a slave, and does not know when or how it has happened. The people around her are not more wicked, more vicious, more detestable than those she has had around her all her life. She just feels their presence around her more. They are ever present, and she starts to do things to please them as if she owed them something, as if she were answerable to them. Answerable for what? They do not ask anything of her, but against all her natural instincts, against her will she strives to give them that something she thinks they expect of her. This forced smile stuck to her face that she hates so much. She feels entangled in thousands of clinging creepers. Fine threads that she ought to be able to shrug off easily, and yet she does nothing.

In the centre of this shrinking spider's web she lies waiting. Waiting for what? Why is she waiting to smash her chains, to take off again? Is she going mad?

Giving up her body is out of the question. Life would no longer have any meaning. His body would feel amputated. Cruelly amputated. If she left him, it would feel like a great claw tearing at his entrails, grubbing for vital organs that it would wrench out to let them trickle from its blood-soaked grasp. Gore. Movies that make you want to throw up. But only too true, too real in Tanaka's mind. Lina is part of his flesh. One of the elements of his flesh. One of the primordial components. Lina is the *sine qua non* of his existence. Lina, Lina's flesh and blood – Tanaka's own flesh and blood. His fuel, his food. . . . Coldly, he tries to reason with himself. How to stop that flesh from being wrenched from his own? He looks blankly at his pencil completely gnawed and torn by his teeth, throws it in the trash-basket and takes a new one.

For Lina, the end of the contract is a nightmare. After a long accumulation of frustrations and daily horrors, an article she read finally decided her to run away. It was a report in a foreign magazine about a ghastly murder that had been committed in Paris by a young Japanese. This crazed youth, after slaughtering a young Dutch girl, had cut her up and eaten certain pieces he had kept fresh in a fridge. Lina reads and rereads the most shocking passages. The realism of the details is revolting. She notices that the fingers holding the magazine are trembling slightly. The article is presented in the form of an interview. The cannibal replies calmly to the journalist's questions, as if it were just a report on some ordinary experience. The images the words evoke in Lina's mind become mixed up with those that have been haunting her for the past weeks, with her nightmares. Deep inside her body something begins to throb dully. That sort of thing often happens to her now. She gets the feeling that a turbine is pounding her soul and all the fibres of her body.

Anything. . . . Anything. . . . He will do anything, as long as she does not leave him!

The throbbing of the great engine gently lulls her to sleep. The slight vibrations that are communicated to her hands on the arm-rests. Behind the veil of her closed eyelids she senses the presence of someone looking at her. With a rather violent start she jerks herself awake and opens her eyes wide to find a face bending over her. 'I'm sorry to have startled you. . . . I just wanted to ask you if you would like a blanket.'

Lina, taking the light blanket that the steward offers her, replies with a reassuring smile. Then, settling down more comfortably, closes her eyes. Calm. Peace. How long has it been since she felt like this? *Happy end.*[32] The nice white hospital, the nice nurses, the clean bandages. In movies, after the journey across the desert, the hell of the battlefield, the thousand dangers of the jungle, the heroes always wake up in this atmosphere of cloistered peace. The viewer breathes more easily. *Happy end.* Lips form a sweet smile on the heroine's face. She has escaped. Why does she think of herself as having escaped? Is she being ridiculous? Ridiculous to have thrown away everything within a few hours. Without goodbyes, without turning back to wave, without thinking, like an automaton. A reflex action. And she will never try to understand why. In a few hours time she will set foot on the soil where she was born. A new life perhaps, a departure. . . . She has to think positively. A departure, that's it. . . . She is entitled to a new departure. To a new life. She looks out of the dazzlingly lit plane window at the majestic ranges of cloud beneath the wide blue yonder. A new life, perhaps . . . or perhaps not.

[32] In English in the French text. The words are a Japanese-English cliché.